CATHERINE **H**UME was born in Norton-on-Tees in 1980, and moved to Blackpool in 1984. While at school, she worked at open-air markets, danced, acted, painted and played tenor trombone in a brass band. During her time at university, in Stoke-on-Trent, she worked in hotels, fast food joints and then with disadvantaged people. Among her favourite experiences she lists standing on top of Whistler's Mountain, Alberta, sand-yachting and finishing this book.

Coming Back to Life

CATHERINE HUME

Steve Savage
LONDON AND EDINBURGH

Steve Savage Publishers Ltd
The Old Truman Brewery
91 Brick Lane
LONDON
E1 6QL

www.savagepublishers.com

Published in Great Britain by Steve Savage Publishers Ltd 2004

ISBN-10: 1-904246-11-7
ISBN-13: 978-1-904246-11-4

British Library Cataloguing in Publication Data
A catalogue entry for this book is available from the British Library

Typeset by Steve Savage Publishers Ltd
Printed and bound by The Cromwell Press Ltd

Contents

For Rosie, Trudi, Lilac, Julie, Heather,
Alastair, Sarah, Ade and Chris

Three Frogs and a Red Bandana

Stoke-on-Trent was sleeping off Friday night, but I was ready for anything.

I sat at my table, reading *The Morning Star*. It was an average summer afternoon. Blazing sun. O'Malley's was run by a guy called John Spencer who fancied himself as a bit of an Irish hero, even though he was born and bred in Burnley. That's maybe why he liked my friend Hepburn so much (with his County Donegal accent, there was no disguising where he came from). Around the café, which became a bar at night, were several people, who sat either alone or in groups round tables. Newspapers were strewn across several of the unoccupied tables. Five musicians were practising their set on the stage—a folk band, who had come to our little hovel of a home in the 'arsehole of Britain', as Stoke-on-Trent is known by people who live outside of the city.

To its residents, though, Stoke-on-Trent is far more than non-residents can imagine. Of course, the city has its problems, especially with the decline of the local pottery industry, which has made so many people unemployed. But, on closer inspection, there are signs of hope, of growth, of rejuvenation and regeneration. Things *can* change.

Parts of Stoke have been known to have a Traveller population, but the city centre was not traditionally known as a breeding ground for socialists and Travellers. However, something had happened there over the last seven months that had caused such people from all over the Midlands to set up house in the city. After the election of a left-wing mayor, the city was seen in a new light by those with rose-tinted spectacles, and with caution by those who knew better. The elected mayor might have spent his life fighting for the underdog, but the BNP had been a close runner-up, and so those with shrewd minds looked upon the city as having a double-edged newness.

I sipped my tea and read my paper, as I did each Saturday afternoon, preparing my mind for the work ahead, which was why a pad and pen were lying on the table as well. Out of the corner of my eye, I saw Hepburn appear from the kitchen, a scarf tied round his long dark hair to keep it from falling into the food, and point in my direction. Several people followed the line of his index finger and stood before my table.

'*Vous êtes Tabitha?*'

I looked up from the paper with a stern glance, for I did not like attention from strangers.

'*Je suis connue comme Tabitha, ouai,*' I responded.

The African man and the two friends accompanying him sat down at my table. The conversation continued, as it had begun, in French, which had alerted me straight away.

'Then you can help us.'

'In what way?'

'In the disappearing sort of a way,' the man replied.

'What's your names?' I asked, just for the sake of convenience—needing to be able to address people is a politeness I do not often ignore in people who deserve my politeness.

'I do not want—'

'Just any names. Doesn't have to be your own.' *Imagination, come on, come on!*

'Er, Jean-Pierre, Luc and Claire.'

'Pleased to meet you,' I replied without smiling. 'Now, what do you want?'

'The Home Office want to send us back to our own country, and we can't go back there,' Jean-Pierre said.

'I gathered that.' I'd met many. 'What country?'

'Congo,' said Jean-Pierre. 'We can't go back.' I saw the desperation in his eyes.

I'd seen it before in countless faces. Of course I would make them disappear. I'd tackle the money issue at a later date.

'You leave here now,' I said, and I saw the sudden look of despair and helplessness on the big man's face, so quickly said all that I had to say, 'and you meet me at 47 Newton Lane at five thirty. Seventeen thirty, understand?'

Jean-Pierre nodded, and rapidly translated in Lingala to his companions. I'd heard those words before several times, so that I was used to recognising which of the twenty-seven Congolese languages was being used. I knew the reasons why people had left Congo, and had known several people sent back there, despite the war continuing, people dying and people torturing. I wonder if you have ever met a woman who has been forced to cook her living husband and watch as the opposing soldiers ate his boiled corpse.

'We will see you then,' Jean-Pierre agreed, as he rose to his feet to leave. The others followed suit. I turned back to my newspaper as the drummer sat on the edge of the stage, and began to adjust the strap on his bodhran.

I let two minutes pass by without event, and then took my mobile phone from my pocket and tapped in a number I knew by heart.

'Hi, it's me, how are you?'

'I'm OK,' Terry said. 'What's up?'

'Three passports and ID—IC3, two males, one female,' I said, using the police's method of describing possible ethnicity. That was the language that Terry worked with in his profession.

'I'll see what I can dig up,' replied Terry, the senior worker at a Birmingham morgue. 'Can you do the photo shoot?'

'I can arrange it. Can you send them up to me by five?'

'You are pushing it, dear,' Terry huffed, letting me know that his ever soaring stress levels were reaching new heights.

'You know I'll love you forever.' He knew that was accurate. Anyone who puts themselves on the line to help people in situations like this has a place in my heart, no matter how hard that heart has become.

'You owe me. I'll send Helena up with whatever I find.' He cut the conversation off.

'Great.' I had asked a great favour, and in return he was sending up someone he knew I despised.

So there I was, at seventeen hundred hours at 47 Newton Lane, a ramshackle mess of a derelict factory in a street of derelict factories. I had left my wallet, watch, jacket and trainers in my room that rested above the bar at O'Malley's. Most exchanges of false ID took place without incident when I dealt with them. Most things I dealt with took place without incident. I treat people well as long as they treat me so. That was why I was wearing my heavy boots, since some people weren't as nice as I was. Helena was one.

The sun was still strong and bright on this summer's evening, and reflected well off the whitewashed walls of the tumbling-down building. I was looking forward to the gathering tonight at O'Malley's. John Spencer's partner, Jenna, had reached the grand old age of thirty, so I was hoping to make it a double celebration, with the knowledge that three people, who could have been sent to their deaths, would soon be happily living in some distant town as British citizens. I flicked a glance at my mobile phone to check the time. Helena was three minutes late. Man, I dislike that woman.

Helena showed at 17:12, with as much flesh on show as possible—as usual. I was not impressed.

'Miss me?' She'd had a new tattoo put on her left arm. Small and aesthetically pleasing.

'Like a bullet in the head. What's he got me?'

'Chill out,' Helena drawled. She knew how to wind me up. 'Have a toke.'

'Just hand the papers over,' I commanded. I knew that Terry was good, but I was still anxious about the suitability of the ID for my Congolese acquaintances.

'Here,' said Helena, taking a plastic A4 wallet from her bag and handing it to me. I took the wallet, inside which were three passports, birth certificates and two drivers' licences.

I shook them out of the wallet to inspect them, and saw that they were good. Two of the birth certificates were French and the other was Belgian. The fact that two of the three appeared to speak little French occurred to me, but as the saying goes, beggars can't be choosers. And the photographs I was arranging would fit nicely into the passports. No one would ever know the difference. My right hand delved into my pocket and I retrieved a small bundle of notes.

'Fifty, hundred, hundred fifty, two hundred, two hundred fifty, three hundred, three fifty, four hundred, four fifty, five hundred, five fifty, six hundred.' I handed the notes to Helena, who put them into her bag.

'So, I'll be seeing you,' Helena said as she turned and walked away.

'Sincerely hope not,' I muttered, putting the paperwork into several of my pockets. Luckily, I had a few.

And thus I waited for the Congolese trio to arrive. I ran my hand against the wall, and the combined dust of the crumbling brick and old white paint came off onto my skin and peppered the air and ground around me.

17:26 and I could hear low voices.

'C'est le lieu? Non, je dois être trompé.'

More whispering followed, panicky and scared. I did not want to reveal myself on the street with them, despite the fact that very, very few people came into this area of town unless they were exchanging money for illegal substances, or were present for some other illegal activity. So I picked up a quarter of a brick that was lying on the ground, and threw it against the wall. The sound echoed down the deserted street and plaster fell off the wall. My hair was now white. But the Congolese came running.

'This is the right place. Don't worry,' I assured them, 'no one knows we're here.'

'Good. We are all very scared,' Jean-Pierre told me. 'We want everything to go smoothly.'

'Yes, we're scared,' Claire emphasised this point again.

'I understand,' I nodded, and began unzipping my pockets. 'Let's get this over and done with as quickly as possible. You still need to get photos. The details are here—'

And so I started to pull the documents from my pockets. The passports and contact details were almost in Jean-Pierre's hands when I heard suddenly:

'Armed police! Stop where you are!'

The air filled with confusion, and my three acquaintances were panicking. Who could blame them? But we needed to keep our heads together.

'*Calmez, calmez!*' I looked around the half-fallen-down building and clapped my eyes on the staircase that led upwards and upwards to what looked to be the remains of a third-storey floor. I saw the open wall of the factory next door—there was probably scope to run through the remains of the rafters of all these buildings and escape. Thank God for firetrap factories.

'I'm giving you a minute to come out of the building with your hands above your head.'

A minute is quite a generous head start. Tugging on Jean-Pierre's coat, and pointing upwards, I said, 'Look! All the factories are connected and in ruins. Run up the stairs and into the next building and continue like that until you reach the end building, and then leave by the back door. I will do my best to hold them off. Explain to the others.'

Jean-Pierre translated the plan to Luc and Claire, who had probably understood most of what I had said, anyway, whilst I shouted to the crowd outside, 'Whatcha gonna do with us?'

The French word for 'crowd' is '*foule*'.

'We will not harm you as long as you lay down your weapons and come out with your hands above your head.'

I saw Jean-Pierre, Luc and Claire look at me. I gave them the rest of the documents and put my index finger to my lips.

'*En silence et la vitesse,*' Claire nodded. '*Nous comprenons. Au revoir.*'

'*Au revoir,*' I said. '*Allez, maintenant!*'

The trio moved quickly up the staircase, not making much sound, but even so it might be heard outside. I needed to cover up their noise. Stealing a look at the gathered mass outside through the window, I saw four police cars and approximately twenty-five armed officers and seven ordinary police officers.

'What'm I supposed to 'ave done?'

'Don't act innocent with us, luv. Come out with your hands above your head. This is the last time we'll ask.'

I ducked beneath the window and crossed the room quietly until I reached the staircase. Slowly and quietly, I began to ascend, keeping my footsteps close to the wall. First floor, second floor approaching.

'Alright, we're coming in.'

The sound of twenty-five armed officers scurrying about on the ground floor was all that I could hear. They were checking the old cupboards and crannies thoroughly. Then the whispering as orders were given. Soft footsteps on the concrete stairs. I waited several seconds, then put my head over the side of the staircase where I was stood. A sharp young lad spotted me and several figures clothed in black with bullet-proof vests ran up the staircase to the first floor. They'd be a minute or two checking that floor. I started to run, too, and stopped on the second floor. Pulling my mobile out of my pocket, I called a saved number. I had been provided with a solicitor to help me with my work.

'Debbie, I'll need you at the nick in about half an hour.'

The phone went back into my pocket and I crouched in the far corner of the room, feigning fear. I always pretended when it came to emotions. All I can remember was a big hand coming towards me and then

———

The door swung open and I stepped into the darkness. Through the narrow walkway, so familiar, so dark. I could hear the noise getting louder and louder and I took another step forward, through the chains of coloured beads, and I was in a different world. The lights were blazing red, blue and yellow, and the bar was packed full of revellers and artists. By the far wall, Aristotle was stood on a box, his face painted black and white to suit his Pierrot clothing, and his hair was scraped back off his face. Around him was colour as he juggled four clubs, one red, one blue, one yellow and one that was flaming. On the stage, a group of young things were performing an Orwell scene, watched by a crowd of people. Sitting with his feet up on the chair in front of him was the intellectual Scottish playwriter and events organiser, dressed in his trademark Doc Martens and a duffle coat, despite the heat in the bar. At the back, sat with friends, was a familiar beach-blonde with stunning make-up and expensive clothes, flicking her hair around and laughing. Kelly seemed relaxed for once. Around the stage in the faces of the guests were intrigue, laughter, awe and happiness.

Leaning on the bar, I gazed in wonder at the sight of so many happy faces that had come from so much strife. At first, I did not notice Hepburn, his hair tied back with a red bandana, standing with a large glass filled to the brim with Baileys Irish Cream.

'Let me tell you a story about three Frogs that hopped all the way to Leeds.' He held out the glass to me.

'No evidence, was there? All circumstantial, those photos of me and three Black faces. Could've been Destiny's Child from the angle they were taken—' and I stopped myself. They were.

Sunny Days

I decided this was a good place to be. The sun was shining brightly, the air was fresh, the view was spectacular and my friend Hepburn was with me. John and his girlfriend Jenna were walking a distance behind us. For a couple of vegetarians, they were *so* unfit. Maybe it's because they normally didn't stray far from the bistro. It was John's birthday, so we'd had a whip-round to send him and Jenna to County Donegal for a week. I had put up most of the money, being the highest earner (and the most grateful to John for letting me lodge at O'Malley's).

Hepburn and I made our way easily over the yellow rocky peninsula that stuck out into the Atlantic Ocean, as we were more physically fit than John and Jenna put together, which wasn't very hard. We raced out, gradually putting quite a distance between the couple and us as we traversed the rocks around the bay. The spray of the sea wet my knee-length khaki shorts and rucksack as we scrambled over the rocks. Hepburn did not know what was in the back compartment of the rucksack. All that he thought I was carrying was what we had packed together for our dinner.

By noon, the well-dressed figures of John and Jenna were nowhere in our sight as we sat on the rocks, looking out across the bay, trying to spot them making their way towards us.

'Maybe they got distracted?' I thought out loud.

'I'm sure we could get distracted, too,' Hepburn said, and answered my questioning look by pointing to a rickety-looking house that was built on some higher rocks beneath a high cliff by a small alcove in the bay. There was a small cave just next to the house and a jetty, and I was naturally curious.

'Come on, then,' Hepburn sighed, standing up, knowing that he had whetted my curiosity, and we made our way towards the cave. My mind twitched as I thought of the papers in the back compartment of my rucksack.

When we reached the cave, I saw that it was only a small opening in the cliff face, and that the sea had worn away the whole cliff, rather than just patches, so the cave was not too deep. I was a little disappointed, but actually, bizarrely, it had been the house itself that had caught my attention, and imagination. There were possibilities entering my mind.

The house was just as ruinous, or maybe even more so, close up as it had seemed previously. The wooden door had rotted on its hinges and hung open, shamefacedly. The windows had been blacked out with thick backing material.

The state that the house seemed to be in and the fact the windows were blacked out made me wonder. Hepburn seemed to know what I was thinking.

'There is a modern legend about the Boyd family,' he said. 'They lived here up until 1943, and then nothing more was heard of them. Some say that the father, Jack, was a spy for the Nazis, which was why he lived out here, away from the town, and some say that there were weird goings on here. There's the odd tale or two, but there's little certainty about anything involving the Boyds.'

'Tell me more about them,' I said, intrigued.

'Well, there were five children: Aidan, Eamonn, Gearóid, and the twins Mahon and Fina,' Hepburn said. 'Jack Boyd and his wife Caroline disappeared in the night, as I said, in 1943, and the kids were put into care. They were all separated for years, but managed to retrace each other and finally were all reunited at the end of the seventies. Mahon is my father.'

I looked back at Hepburn, who was looking at me in a direct sort of a way, and he said, 'I wanted to bring you here. It's the first time I've been here, to retrace my family's steps. So I'm looking forward to digging around in this old place for a while.'

Hepburn led the way into the house, pushing past the rotted door and into the hallway of the house. Part of the actual hallway floor was submerged under an inch of water that had flowed in from the sea and become trapped.

I suppose that when the house was in use, the door would have been in working order and water-proofed, so this would not have been a problem for Hepburn's grandparents.

The floor itself was made up of small red tiles, all still hammered and glued into place, just like the red and cream tiles that lined the walls, where there were shelves laden with small brass jugs and plates and other small artifacts from prewar times. There were two rooms leading off to the right, and three to the left.

The two at the front appeared to serve as a nursery and a sitting room, the one at the back righthand side of the house was an adult's bedroom with medical articles such as a catheter and equipment for the sterilisation of hypodermic needles in plain view. There were two needles in a ceramic pot by the window. Whoever had been sterilising them had meant to use them again, which raised the question, what happened to the user of the needles, who was obviously so ill?

As I moved towards the back of the left side of the house, which led into the kitchen area, something about the wall by the hallway fireplace caught my eye. The kitchen itself was quite extensive, but then it would have needed to be to act as a food preparation space and dining area for five children and two adults. Besides that, the storage area would have been bigger than its modern counterparts because the geese and chickens would have had to have taken shelter there at night. There was still straw scattered across the kitchen floor. I was surprised that the elements hadn't disturbed more of the house's contents over the decades. Why was that? And why wasn't there a layer of dust on top of everything? This wasn't right.

'Hepburn! Hepburn!'

'I'm out the front,' he said. 'And keep your voice down.'

I splashed a little through the water of the hallways and stumbled over fragments of the rot that had fallen off the door.

'What's going on here?'

'Someone's been here,' Hepburn said. 'But they're not here any more.'

'You don't say.'

'She's dead.' Hepburn gave me a look.

'Who?'

'I think she might be my grandmother,' he replied. 'Fina and Eamonn have a real look of her—the woman upstairs.' He shook his head with apparent sadness and said, 'I never thought I'd meet her, but I thought that coming here would provoke something.

'Like what?'

Hepburn shrugged.

'I don't know.' He smiled wanly. 'It was just a feeling I had. But I can't believe this. To find her here, like this.' He shook his head again in confusion.

This situation would bamboozle *any*one. Situations must be so much harder when they are family-related.

'I've never even spoken with her, and now I find her like *this*.' He became quiet and thoughtful.

I did not know how to help him, so I asked him, 'Was she alone?'

This was a difficult thing for Hepburn, I knew, but all I could deal with was facts.

'Yes, she was alone, and it looks like she lived upstairs for the time she was here. It doesn't look like she had been back long. Maybe a few days. There's two changes of clothes on the floor. I reckon she spent most of the time in the bedroom,' Hepburn said. 'There was a TV, kettle and bits of food and fruit. That way she wouldn't have to keep going up and down stairs.'

'So she starved to death?' It was a horrible thought.

'No,' Hepburn smiled. 'It looks like she knew she was dying—her body is very frail—and she came back here somehow. Maybe someone brought her? I don't know. But she had written something.'

'What?'

Hepburn had in his hand a piece of paper that I noticed now. He looked at it and read what he could.

'"*Cronaim*", er, "*grá mo chroí*", that means "I miss", and then it's smudged, and then it says "love of my heart", so she might be talking about my grandfather.' Hepburn squinted at the page, where I could see the ink had run. Perhaps the old lady had been crying, perhaps she had spilt water on the page.

Hepburn continued, '"*Ar dheis Dé go raibh a anam a Rí na mblat is na mbreth*", "may his soul be on the right side of God, O King of might and judgment".'

Hepburn looked up. 'It seems like my grandmother was a woman of faith. Perhaps my grandfather screwed up somehow?'

I nudged him and said, 'Carry on.'

'The rest is really blurred,' he said. '"*Gellaí*"—that's "promise" and "*scél*" means "story", but I can't make any of the rest out, except more declarations of faith and love for someone, probably my grandfather. It sounds like she's making a promise to tell her story, but why would she have written the promise down?'

'Maybe she wanted someone else to know?' I suggested.

'Then why come back here?' Hepburn wondered. 'Why not just go and tell someone or stay with someone, instead of being out here all alone? I'm sure she knew she was dying.'

'Maybe this place is familiar?' I offered. 'But something *is* odd about this to me.'

'Oh yeah?' Hepburn looked at me, asking with his eyes.

'First, your gran comes back here alone in her dying days. How? And why? Second, you come out here on holiday just days after. Is that a coincidence?'

'I don't believe in coincidence,' Hepburn said.

'Neither do I,' I said, but probably for different reasons to Hepburn. 'Did anyone else know that we were coming out here?'

'No, because we're staying up the coast,' Hepburn said. 'We only came here because I decided to last night. And besides, my grandmother and I have different surnames, due to my father being in care. Even if someone else had known that I was coming here, they would never have related me to my grandmother.'

'Then how could all this have happened in such a short space of time?' I asked.

'I don't know,' Hepburn said, putting the paper into the back of my rucksack. 'I'll have a think about it.'

We left the old house and continued to walk to the picnic site in silence, just like when we had been scrambling over the rocks. I was busy taking in the beauty of nature, amazed at how the gulls' feathers gleamed brilliant white in the sun's strong rays. I was sure that Hepburn's mind was busy, working his way through the letter again and again in his mind, trying to find a meaning in the Irish words, and a meaning behind the 'coincidences'.

Hepburn sat down on the picnic table bench under a clump of fir trees, sheltered from the sun, and the pine cones under his foot scrunched and crunched and crumbled as he made himself comfortable. I joined him, and dug in the rucksack for the Cornish pasties and apples. It was strange that John and Jenna had not yet arrived at the picnic site. I looked down at the ground, and in between the pine cones were small insects, beetles, creeping around, and crawling over each other.

'So, have you reached any conclusions, Sherlock?' I asked in between mouthfuls of pasty. Hepburn nodded and made noises as he chewed and swallowed pastry.

'Yes,' he cleared his throat. 'I believe this is all about you. It all happened for you.'

'What?' I coughed up some pastry in a lump that landed on the ground in front of me. The insects made a beeline for it. Hepburn slapped me lightly on the back. It wasn't the part of my back that's sensitive. He knew that.

When I had reassured him that I was OK, he continued.

'My grandmother came back to the family house and tried to write about what had happened, but death got in the way of her finishing what she had started,' he said. 'So we'll never know. But,' he said with emphasis, 'I think there's a greater force at work here, who wants you to start writing about where you've been and what you've seen.'

I spluttered, laughing.

'You what?!'

'Don't laugh, Tabitha,' Hepburn said. 'You've had a very unique life and seen things that other people wouldn't even dream of—'

'Or have nightmares about.'

'And the sort of things you find out in your, um, work,' Hepburn continued, 'I think you need to start sharing them with the rest of the world. There's something special about you and your life. I'm sure of it.'

'I wish people would stop telling me that.'

'You've heard that before?' Hepburn picked up on this.

'Yeah, in Spain, in South Carolina, here and there, people I've met, people I've known.' I was sick of it.

'I think it's something you should pay heed to,' Hepburn said.

I was used to Hepburn being right about things. I wanted to question his judgment on this issue, but somehow I couldn't. I didn't want him to be right. I didn't want to be 'special'.

'Where are they?' I stood up and looked around for John and Jenna. They were nowhere to be seen. I was already worried. Hugely. I always worried about everyone who knew me. I didn't want anything bad to happen to them.

'I think we'd better go and have a look for them,' Hepburn said, calmly. He was always calm. I'm sure he was still affected by everything around him, but he never panicked. Not like me.

We put the apples back into the rucksack, which I slung into place on my back, and made our way out of the picnic site and we began to retrace our steps, as if we had lost an earring.

It was half an hour later when we found John and Jenna. On the rocks, just by the alcove in the bay by Hepburn's grandparents' house. A trawler boat, painted light blue, had stopped by the jetty, and I recognized the captain's face. Well, I recognised his brown woollen jumper first—the one he had been wearing when cooking the breakfast this morning at the guest house, with several holes in the arms. He was the owner of the guest house we were staying at.

Hepburn and I scrambled over the rocks and splashed through shallow pools to reach John and Jenna, wondering what was wrong. Why was Mr Connors coming to pick them up in his boat? I turned to Hepburn and asked quickly, 'Should we tell them about what—I mean who—we found?'

'No,' he replied. 'This is John's holiday, and besides, I'll need to speak to my family, and then the *Gardaì*. Just pretend we haven't seen anything yet. But I'll go back. I can't leave her to decompose in the bedroom.'

'Hey!' I called over to the wayward couple, waving, and climbed up the set of rocks that led across the alcove to the jetty.

'Oh hi!' Jenna gushed, bending forward to greet me, careful in her pricey skirt and pink flip-flops. She waved to Hepburn, who was just behind me.

'What's up?'

'Oh!' Jenna was laughing. 'I'm so unfit!'

She laughed again in that blonde girly way of laughing. It went through me like plastic scraping at ice.

'We're getting a bit lazy, like,' John explained. He stroked his beard. 'And a bit lost, so we called Mr Connors here to come and get us.'

For crying out loud! Mr Connors has better things to be doing.

But I couldn't say that to John, who had been so good to me.

After John had climbed into the boat, he helped Jenna to step over the starboard bow and called over, 'Are you coming back with us?'

'Nah,' I said. 'I think I'll stay here.' I had been thinking. I had seen something in the house that had caught my interest. 'I'll come back in my own time.'

'Yeah, I'll have a look around here,' Hepburn said. I knew he would have to make arrangements to have his grandmother's body removed and taken to the morgue until the funeral could take place. It would take even longer if there was to be an investigation into the old lady's death. But she was an old lady. Maybe that would be sufficient for the coroner? I had to think, and came up with a plausible excuse:

'I'll go and have a tidy up.'

That seemed to convince him. She was dead. She wasn't going to need the house any more. And it would be a while before Hepburn would sort out the paperwork for the sale of the house. Maybe he would keep it, as some families tended to do. This would be a good place to escape to.

We both went into the house, and I went to the kitchen to pretend to tidy up the straw as Hepburn took out his mobile phone and asked the operator to put him in touch with the local *Gardaí*. I heard him relaying his discovery of his deceased grandmother to the *Gardaí* over the phone, and I went to my rucksack. I would have enough time.

I crouched in the hallway and took the documents out from my rucksack, in their plastic bag, and pushed them behind the gap in the cracked wall of the chimney that I had noticed earlier. There they would stay until I was ready to retrieve them.

'What're you doing?'

Hepburn was behind me.

'Just looking at the coal grid.' I hated lying to him. It was the first time, and the last.

He looked at me with suspicion, knowing that I didn't do anything without reason. I couldn't just be curious. But he didn't have a clue, so I felt more at ease.

'Time to go,' he said, and I followed without any delay, on my best behaviour.

The journey back to England went without anything notable happening, but I was exhausted the following day, and had spent most of the day sleeping. I got up in time for tea, and went downstairs to O'Malley's, where Hepburn was serving food to students and well-meaning types. I ordered potato and chillie and slumped at my usual table, which was set for dining, and waited for the food to arrive.

In between waiting on a table and going back to the kitchen, Hepburn came over to my table and sat down opposite me.

'Hello, Sleepy.'

'Hi,' I replied from under an arm that was somehow keeping my head propped up from a particularly weird angle.

We sat in silence for several moments, until I began to feel something. It had started happening in the last two weeks. I hated it. An enormous sensation of anger swept over me, starting in my stomach, and swirling up my throat, with tendrils curling around my brain.

I let out a yell, and hurled the salt cellar across the room so that it smashed against a wall above a table where a man was sat reading the paper.

'Get her out of here, now!'

John had run out from the kitchen and jumped over the bar, and was pointing at me, and suddenly seemed much older than twenty-nine, in his pressed trousers and blue shirt with its sleeves rolled up to the elbows. His beard gave him an air of authority, too. Hepburn made a move to grab my wrists, but I swung around and sulked out of the bistro instead. John was standing by the bar, and did not look impressed. I was sat on the stairs and heard John say to Hepburn:

'Sort her out. I can't let that happen again.'

'I'll try.'

I wanted Hepburn to try. So when he came over to me and sat next to me on the staircase, and asked what had made me act like that, I said, 'Nothing,' and walked out, slamming the door.

The sun was bright outside, making the dull street seem light and not so dirty. The sun shines on the good and bad, and the rain falls on the good and bad, as I'd heard Hepburn say in the past, which is why he accepts people as they are. He said he did not have the right to judge. I wondered if I was good or bad.

Bombay Duck

It had been a long, bad day so far, and it was going to get worse.

The station was quite lively for a Monday morning. Of course, there were plenty of commuters, off to work in Manchester for the day, where the money and jobs were, and then they would come back to Stoke later on tonight and feed their children. Or their fish.

I was standing in the general area of the station, the modern bit, rebuilt a year after the firebomb had burnt down most of the edifice, thus making it necessary for the ticket vendors to operate out of a Portakabin for a year. However, the station now had a renewed feeling about it, and had had the honour of Her Majesty the Queen opening the First Class lounge. How delightful for us mere mortals.

However, the Queen did see more of Stoke-on-Trent. Having travelled behind black windows up the ramshackle route known as Stoke Road, HM had the honour of opening the new theatre in the Cultural Quarter, and then took a spin down Hope Street (remember the song?), which is a desperate place, to open the Dudson Centre. The Dudson, however, is a great innovative thing, born out of a hopeless mess of a closed pot bank—one of the establishments that created the pottery that once had made Stoke-on-Trent world famous. It has reopened as an urban renewal centre, complete with housing advisers, drugs workers and counsellors.

So, standing underneath the grand new arches of Stoke station, I watched as people walked through the automatic doors and out, and walked on past me. I was a bit nervy, having submitted several pieces of information to contacts on the internet the day before. Sunday was a day of flaming hard work for me, spent in one of the many computer rooms of Staffordshire University, just round the corner from the train station. Good place, good people, good facilities, of which I took advantage with my year's pass to the university. The computer technicians assumed I was merely an out-of-work graduate. Little did they know. I'm like a Bombay duck. I'm not what people think I am, yet I never pretend to be something that I'm not (when I'm not pretending to be someone else, that is).

I saw that the train to Manchester Piccadilly would be seven minutes late. That gave me time to collect a newspaper and peruse the day's news. My bag was heavy on my shoulders, full of documents for my three contacts. I descended the steps of the subway and ascended the other side. Facing the track, I stood with my back resting against the chocolate-dispensing machine with a bag strap in my right hand and the newspaper in my left. The other people on the platform were all businessmen and women, in their pinstripes, accompanied by briefcases. I saw the way two of the men looked at me. They looked down on me. My appearance was different to theirs, with my dreadlocked hair, blue Doc Martens, brown combat trousers and unbuttoned blue corduroy shirt revealing a neck-high black T-shirt.

'The train now arriving on platform two is for Manchester Piccadilly, stopping at Kidsgrove, Macclesfield, Stockport and Manchester Piccadilly. Manchester Piccadilly on platform two.'

I hauled my bag back onto my back and stood on the edge of the platform, watching, along with everyone else, the train snake along the track with a seemingly delayed slowness that was unreal. The red-and-white whooshed into the station. I was standing back by the chocolate machine again, not only to prevent myself from being dragged under the train's path, but in shock and distress. They were there, on the other platform.

How did they know? Will they never give up?

As the train came to a standstill, I wrenched open a difficult door and shut it behind me. My stomach jumped when it opened again and two businessmen got in and shut the door after themselves. I stood there, by the door, looking at the entrance of the subway by the chocolate machine. The guard's whistle sounded and the train lurched forward, then slowly began to pick up speed.

Please don't, please don't.

They were on the platform. The train was going too fast for them to catch hold of a door handle. I watched them as they stood stranded. Still holding my breath, I took a seat in the Quiet Coach. I chose a seat opposite a thin guy, who wore huge green-brown corduroy trousers and a T-shirt which had a picture of a spade printed on the front. I offered his colourfully-dressed girlfriend my newspaper, which she shared with him. Still keeping a hold of my bag, I sat back in the seat and closed my eyes. Peace.

The train approached Manchester Piccadilly with velocity, as usual. I was stood by the door, with my head out of the window, feeling the wind against my face and hearing the expectation in my heart. The train slowed and eventually stopped on the familiar platform, which was inhabited by people with trolleys and suitcases and toddlers and helium balloons. As soon as I was out of the door, I was running. Out of the glass automatic doors and up the escalator to the fast food bar.

And there he was. Dave sat at the second to last table. His brown jacket was matted with dirt, his hair was uncombed and his fingernails blackened. I had known that the journalist was feeling worse than usual, but I had not expected things to be this bad. I sat down opposite him and took my bag off quickly.

'How's things?'

'So-so,' he replied, as downbeat as ever. With Dave, the glass was always more than half empty. 'Work's been slow lately.' He drank from a polystyrene cup that contained black coffee.

'Well, here, have this,' I said as I handed him one of the files from my bag. 'You'll love this.'

'Where did you get it all from?' Dave said, perusing the subheadings. 'The Private Finance Initiative's all new stuff. How do I know this is all reliable and not just opinion?'

'Take a look at some of the sources.' I pointed to the second page. 'PFI could bleed the UK dry. That PFI hospital in Carlisle. Cost around eighty-seven million and it's riddled with faults. And look at this PFI school in Wales. Built on a toxic waste site. Go on, have a right good look.'

'I will do, at home,' Dave put the file into his own bag, which was battered and had seen better days. 'How's things with you?'

'Busy.' I answered. 'I've had a time promoting a folk band a Stokie called Hepburn is getting together with his mate Danny.' I glanced at my watch. 'Look, I'm sorry, but I've got to go. I've got two more people to see today. I zipped up my bag as I stood up, and put it on my shoulders ready for the next sprint.

'See you around.' Dave glanced up from his coffee.

'And my payment?'

'The cheque's in the post,' said Dave without a hint of humour.

I looked him in the eye, for I had suddenly lost all my sense of humour, too.

'Better be.'

Dave looked at the coffee again. I put my right foot forward and started to run.

Forwards, past the fast food counter, beyond the posh café and down the escalators. I had to be at Piccadilly Gardens ten minutes ago.

I stood, breathing heavily, on the bridge, surrounded by flying water. Skater kids hung out beyond the bridge on the concrete step by the curved walls. It wasn't fair. They were having fun in the sun. And I was late. Maybe I'd missed her. Maybe that's it, and that's half of this month's income down the toilet. Maybe I think too much.

Alenska Deschamps turned around and walked towards me. She was six feet two inches tall, with long natural blonde hair and a slim build. Alenska always dressed in expensive garments, very tasteful and respectable. She swept along the bridge, her three-quarter-length fawn coat flapping in the breeze, the brown stiletto heels accentuating every step harshly. Alenska was not a woman who like to be kept waiting, though she did not show it in her demeanour. She just docked money from the pay packet.

'Janey, so nice to see you again,' Alenska gushed as she embraced my reluctant body and caught a fingernail on the zip of my bag. She pushed me away to examine her nail and then looked at me in an accusing manner.

'Sorry,' I said. 'Did it hurt?'

'No. I have to rush, darling,' Alenska was not pleased. 'Do you have what I want?'

'Here or—?'

'Down there.' She pointed to Lever Street, and I started to walk beside her in that direction. The top half of Lever Street was usually crowded and is quite a trendy place to be seen, but as you go further down the road, it gets more and more deserted as the shops get less trendy and more scruffy and cheap and closed. Very few people go far down that road or the roads around it, and at night-time it's not the best place in the world to be. That's where Alenska was taking me.

I tried my best to keep up the pretence of wanting to be sociable. 'So, how's the job going?'

'Well,' the tall Slavic-French woman replied in her neutral accent. 'I'm just trying to work my way up the ladder. Kissing the satan's balls to do it, but it's worth it.'

She wanted my interest.

'Oh yes?'

'I've been given a chance by an international paper to do an exposé on a gangland boss who's big in Europe. If I pull it off, I get a job. If I don't, I might as well slash my own wrists as far as my career is concerned.'

I didn't understand these things. 'I get it.'

'I doubt it,' Alenska smiled. She stopped in the middle of the pavement and three young Asian men swerved past, narrowly avoiding bumping into us. 'Now, where's my goody bag?'

I took the bag from my back and took out the blue folder. 'All the facts on asylum seekers, the HIV infection rate and whatever else in between.' Alenska took the folder from me, stuffed it inside her small handbag, which was then secured back onto the epaulette of her coat.

'I think that concludes our little tête-à-tête,' Alenska said. Her smile had become broader. She disliked associating with a scruffy female who lived on the margins of society, which is what she saw me as, even though she needed me.

I clicked my fingers and held out my hand.

Alenska gave a tiny laugh. 'I'm a silly billy, aren't I? Here.' And she handed me the cash, with fifty pounds missing because I had kept her waiting for fourteen minutes. And I was so grateful.

'Till next time.' I turned around and walked away from her. It was time to take a walk and then go and see my next and final client. Unlike the other two, this next person was someone I actually like and socialise with whenever possible. It was unfortunate that we were only 'ships passing in the night' today.

Jason is always late. I don't mind, though, especially since he's my last port of call today. I could never mind with Jason; he's too lovely to get angry at. I stood with my back against the wall outside of the main entrance to the three-floored alternative market. Jason loved the café on the top floor.

'Hi, am I late?'

I just grinned and walked into the market and up the stairs. Jason did all the talking, which is how I prefer things. He talked for quite a while, knowing that he could speak openly to me, and did not stop even when we had seated ourselves in the café. We looked an odd pair, I knew that. Jason was dressed in his drainpipe trousers and a stripy blazer, and was waving his hands about, and talking in an animated, camp manner. I sat opposite, hardly moving, slouched with my legs apart, as a man would, taking in all my friend was saying.

'Guess what I've got for you?' I said after Jason had finished pouring out his heart and we were devouring our puddings.

'Twenty thousand pounds?'

'Fraid not.' I winked and pulled a red folder from my bag. 'A present from me to you.' I handed him the folder.

Without looking, Jason asked, 'What's in it?'

'Information. All you need to get a few rungs up the ladder for a while.'

'What sort of information? I hope you didn't go to a load of trouble for little me.' Jason was genuine in his modesty, although he had ambition.

'You know, just some hot potatoes, like PFI, asylum seekers in relation to AIDS, asylum-seeker figures, HIV/AIDS rates in the UK, and surprise, surprise, the majority are heterosexual British women.'

'But Ann, what am I supposed to do with this?' Jason looked up from the reams of paper. I took a deep breath and exhaled.

'Write,' I replied. 'Now, take a look at what I've dug up to do with PFI: the Chancellor of the Exchequer is quoted as saying here'—I pointed to an underlined sentence on the first page—'that he does not care what the experts say: he's going ahead with PFI no matter what. Class stuff.'

'Oh yeah, I've heard bits and bobs about that,' Jason interjected. 'The hospitals are smaller, so they've got less beds, less equipment and less staff.' He got out a biro and a scrap of paper from the back pocket of his trousers and began scrawling notes. 'But I can see how private firms running buildings could be to the advantage of the taxpayer, you know, with the private firms paying for the overheads.'

'Yeah, I get that,' I said, 'but I do think this "mortgaging" of schools and hospitals is a concern for Britain. Read the rest yourself, but it's something that's bugging me the more I read about it.'

I handed him the folder and zipped my bag up. Jason looked up meekly from his scrawling.

'You've gone to so much trouble for me,' he said.

'No, it wasn't much extra work,' I assured him.

Jason looked bewildered. 'I don't know what to say.'

'Don't say anything, and I mean not a word, but just do something with it.'

'Ann, thank you,' Jason said as he put the folder into his bag, carefully. 'Thank you. I'm sorry. I have to go.'

'I know. It's OK. Just go and see Jill and have a good evening with her.'

Jason stood up and bent over to kiss my cheek. 'I will. It's her night off from the unit tonight.' Jason kissed me again. 'You're great. Thanks,' and he ran out of the door.

I slurped the bottom of my milkshake and didn't care when two girls stared.

The board showed that the train back to Stoke would leave in two minutes' time.

I had more than enough time to get to Platform 6, so I sauntered casually up to the train and took a seat in the Quiet Coach. A man with a briefcase and a pinstriped suit sat opposite me and opened a battery-powered laptop. I retrieved a thick novel from my bag and was about to start reading as the train pulled away from the platform slowly. But something caught my eye. Black. Black, and more figures dressed in black running along the platform, keeping level with my window. It was them again.

What was this? Why were they here as well as Stoke? If they wanted me, then why didn't they get me before I got on the train? And why were they being so open in a very crowded area? I just couldn't escape them. It didn't make any sense. *It just doesn't make sense.*

Please. Please.   Please.

They did not attempt to board the train. Why? Why? I tried to swallow the panicky pain that had lodged itself in my throat, and eventually, it went back down to the back of my mind where it lived surreptitiously. I opened my book and read.

The door opened with a creak. It needed oiling, and I'd avoided doing so for several weeks now. I stuck my head around the door to the bar and saw that there were quite a lot of people in tonight. There was a group of middle-aged people who were dressed in sensible clothes. I think they must have been on a works night out and mistakenly walked through O'Malley's front door, thinking it was a place for 'normal' people to go to. They were looking in distaste at the pink dreadlocks of the girl on the table next to them, but seemed to enjoy the folk music that was being played by a live three-piece band on the stage, although I think the anarchism of the lyrics would have escaped them. I walked up to the bar, leaving my bag in the hallway.

'The usual?' Ben was serving behind the bar tonight. He was a new employee, tall, thin and ginger, who had just come from Edinburgh. His story was a complex lie, but he had been honest in his work so far, so there was no reason to sack him. He fitted in well, with blue and white woven jumper and camouflage trousers, and an easy-going attitude.

'I think so. It's been a long one today. I was up at five, printing some stuff out.'

Ben handed me a glass half full of Baileys, and I was about to go upstairs to my room when Hepburn appeared from the kitchen.

'Not so fast,' he said, with a guitar in his hand. 'The band's finishing in a mo, and I need a beautiful young woman to serenade, but I guess I'll have to make do with you.'

'Oh no,' I moaned. 'Please, just let me go to bed and be miserable.'

'Nope, it's hot lights and stage fright for you, my dear,' he said as he stepped out from behind the bar and took hold of my hand. I let him lead me across the floor of the venue and we sat on the edge of the stage as he sang to me, enthralling some of his fans in the audience. They were the regulars who came every Monday night and stayed until closing time, just to hear Hepburn play a few songs.

As he sang to me, I thought of Jason, out with his girlfriend. He is a good lad, with a big future ahead of him. If only he could see that and chase after it. Jason is sweet and timid, yet he has an important choice to make: he can either go with the flow and get swallowed up by the tide, or he can cling to what is right. I remembered the smile on his face, and that made me smile. And I thought of him writing a bigger scoop than Dave and Alenska put together, two of the top journalists in Manchester. And that made me content. It had been a good day.

I Wish

'Tabitha, post for you.'

'I'll be out in a minute, Ben,' I called back to him. I hauled my cargo trousers on, ensuring the zips were closed, and then I opened my bedroom door. Ben's hair was still dishevelled from the night before, and he was wearing his boxers and freckles with weariness.

'You should've stayed in bed,' I told him.

'I need the money,' Ben replied.

'Stuff the money, you're wrecked.'

'We're not all as sought-after as you,' Ben said, which made me cringe inside. He had no idea. He went on, 'Some of us have to work our butts off to make ends meet. Anyway, here's your post.'

'Thanks,' I snatched the two envelopes from his outstretched hand and slammed my bedroom door. I grabbed my big, funky red, unisex trainers from the bottom of the wardrobe, careful to not dislodge the arrangement of clear plastic wallets that contained documents of research and Indian rupees.

As I tugged on a pair of socks and the trainers, I heard shouting. I couldn't distinguish the words, but the tone was violent, and seemed to shake the warehouse.

I put the memory aside and made my way down to the bistro quietly. Ben and I were the only two awake, as it was our turn to open up. Everyone else was sleeping off the night before. O'Malley's had been open until four o'clock this morning as we had been commemorating the D-Day Landings and celebrating everything that meant. Four veterans had even honoured us with their presence, having heard of our night of celebration, and they had left me in awe. I hadn't been able to talk to them, but they still amazed me. I felt very privileged.

Going to the effort of hardly making a sound as I tiptoed along the hallway, then down the stairs—keeping close to the wall affected me. As I inhaled, a stress pain hit my stomach. It had reminded me of the past—of hiding.

Downstairs in O'Malley's, I left the two envelopes behind the bar for later, and began to take down the chairs from the tabletops. Ben was quietly clattering away in the kitchen, setting out crockery and preparing the plates of scones and slices of cakes. The metal teapots stood alert with their lids open on their hinges, ready for the customers who were guaranteed to pile into O'Malley's at eleven o'clock.

I went to the kitchen to get a wet cloth with which I would wipe down the tables. Ben turned around from where he was standing at the counter with a knife and lettuce.

'Tabitha, have you seen the soda bread?' he asked.

'In the *frigo sous l'escalier*,' I replied, without looking up from where I was crouching by the open cupboard under the sink.

'In the where?'

'Sorry.' I realised my mistake. I took a cloth, stood up and closed the cupboard door and repeated, 'In the fridge under the stairs.'

'Are you OK?' Ben asked.

'*Je le souhais*,' I replied and walked off with the wet cloth. I took the two envelopes with me and kept them in my right hand as I wiped the tables down with the blue cloth. Things would have been different if I had been different and allowed to live in the country I was born in. But life had happened, politics had happened. I miss Marseille.

At the final table by the stage, I threw down the cloth and flopped down into the chair I always took. The first envelope was torn open with ease, and I read the contents, enraged.

I retrieved my mobile phone from the deep left pocket of my cargo trousers, and dialled the number at the top of the letter. It took over two minutes for my call to come to the front of the queue.

'Good morning, Elite Catalogue, Malcolm speaking, how can I help you?'

'I just got an offer letter from your company,' I told the man, trying to hold most of my thunder back. It was not his fault. 'Where did you get my name and address from?'

'We would have got your name from a commercial list other companies would have access to,' the kind man replied.

'Well, I don't know how, because this is a completely false name,' I said. 'So I don't know how on earth someone could have passed this name on. Can you remove it from your records now?'

'It will take two weeks to process your request, madam,' the man said, 'but I'll start the ball rolling now. What's your name?'

'The name your company wrote to me?' I asked. 'Tabitha Meera.'

'Can you spell that for me?'

'T-A-B-I-T-H-A-M-E-E-R-A.' I emphasised every letter with impatience, wondering how a person could be so ignorant.

'Right, that's initiated, Miss Meera. Perhaps you'll go back to ordering goods with us again in the future?'

'I don't think so,' I said and pressed the button to hang up, seething. The letter from Elite Catalogue was then quickly ripped up and left in a pile on the table, and I hesitated with the second envelope, as each seam was taped down with black masking tape. I inhaled as I attempted to open it, smelling for anything noxious. Someone had gone to a lot of effort to make sure this envelope was as tightly-wrapped as Tutankhamen.

Eventually, I managed to rip the thick envelope apart and a small note in neat, familiar handwriting fell out. I held the yellow paper between my fingers and thumb, and read the exquisite writing in black ink.

I bet two dollars you are thinking something along the lines of, 'No way!' I'm back and gonna be doing something with that stuff you stashed for me. Every news journal from Alaska to Alabama will be carrying my name. I'll meet you on the 11:51 departing London Euston on Wednesday of the British holiday week.

Oyster Catcher

Oh no. I like Oyster Catcher. He's a good man who had crossed my path due to a mutual acquaintance. I remember the 'stuff' I had kept safe for him. It looked like Congress must be going ahead with their plans to patent mammals and plants, and the Oyster Catcher was going to blow the lid on it and its consequences before it hit the statute books. He thinks it's a bit cheeky for a drugs company to patent, say, the DNA of a dandelion, and have exclusive rights on all dandelions everywhere, so that when dandelions are used in medication, the company can charge as much money as it likes for this natural product. That's basically the top and bottom of it.

A quick trip to County Donegal was on the cards to retrieve the information I had hidden in the cracked chimney of the Boyd family house.

My body froze

as I looked down at the red-and-white chequered tablecloth with the small vase of orange day lilies on it. I called over to the African-American lady in the pink dress at the counter. 'Another cafetière of coffee and a sandwich, please Hetty.'

'Coming right up, Miss May-Louisa.'

I continued to tap away softly on the keys of my laptop as the Tennessee Band played in the street outside. It was a hot July day, and the schools were out. Hetty was busy serving kids ice cream and soda, taking the pocket money they were eager to give.

I came here almost every day, and spent most of the day working on the laptop or reading up on new material and international news. Hetty thought that I could read several languages due to a private education. Despite not telling Hetty about my past, and making up some elaborate lies about my 'private education', we got on and spent some considerable time together. She was fun, with an opinion on everyone, with little time for anything that happened outside of Clemson. To Hetty, the people in this town were the world.

After half an hour, the cafetière arrived, a little shaky and splashed onto the saucer below, and Hetty sat down at my table. I closed my laptop and we peered out of the window together. The band had started to march towards the park, led by a jovial, elderly man, Mr Richards, in a navy-blue, long-tailed coat and trousers, a crisp white shirt that gleamed in the sun, and a blue bow-tie with red glitter. He bobbed from side to side as he walked, waving his navy-blue parasol with red glitter this way and that.

Clemson had a lazy feel about it. As the band disappeared out of sight through the park's gates, followed by families with what seemed like scores of kids, Hetty turned to me and smoothed down her dress.

'Tell me, May-Louisa,' she said, 'why do you insist on wearing those long skirts and tops of yours in this fine weather? You have the figure to be a little less, uh, conservative, with your clothes.'

'Hetty Johnson,' I drawled in my deep southern accent, 'you keep trying to trick and flatter me into confessing all, and it's something I just will not do.' I smiled.

'So you admit there's something to confess,' the old woman deduced, and she lowered her voice and said, 'I've met girls like you before, May-Louisa. Something terrible happened to you, didn't it, child?'

'I don't think you've ever met anyone like me before.' I smiled again at the woman I called 'my friend'.

'May-Louisa, just become you come from money, it don't mean you ain't human.'

Hetty was trying.

'It's not what you think, Hetty,' I said. 'It's my prerogative to dress how I please. And it's also my prerogative to keep an air of mystery around me.'

'Hell, it gives the men something to think about,' Hetty said. 'And that Lucas Jones boy is definitely thinking!'

But I wasn't thinking about Lucas Jones. Besides, I had much more on my mind than matters of the heart.

'So, do you have any plans for tonight?' Hetty asked with innocence.

I could not tell her, even though she was the closest thing I had to a friend.

'This and that,' I said. My eyes wandered to the right and out through the window, until I pulled them back, sharply.

I took hold of Hetty's hand, and almost pleaded, 'Hetty, will you stay with me until my father arrives?'

'What's the matter?' Hetty asked. 'Yes, of course I'll stay. What's wrong?'

'Nothing,' I replied. 'I just think some time with friends is sacred.'

Hetty gave me one of her looks. One of the ones where she knew I was telling the truth, but nowhere near the whole truth.

Hetty stayed with me for four hours. We hardly spoke at some points, and other times we roared with laughter.

The Oyster Catcher appeared in the doorway of Dinah's Diner, and did not remove his hat. Hetty got up.

'She's in one funny mood, Mister Henry, sir,' she told the Oyster Catcher. 'You need to be spending more time with her. She's at risk of turning into one sad tomato.'

'I don't think that will be possible for the foreseeable future, Miss Hetty,' he replied, and then he sat down opposite me.

'I'm glad you're here,' I said.

'Snap out of it. Start acting normal.' he smiled at me.

'I like this place.' I smiled back, holding his hand. 'I don't want to up sticks and leave again, Daddy.'

'But Precious, you must realise that Daddy is going away on business, and you'd better make yourself invisible, my girl, for your own sake,' he responded. 'I do actually care what happens to you, you know?'

'Daddy, your accent's slipping back into that New York way of talking,' I told him.

'Thanks.' he squeezed my hand. 'I'd better practise some.'

He started to lay out the plan.

'So we'll reconvene outside the Institute of Science just by the parking lot.'

'Yes,' I said. 'I'll be the one in the white labcoat.'

The Oyster Catcher looked at me.

I elaborated, 'And the blonde wig and the yellow sweater.'

'The red Buick will be parked up by the grassy verge?'

'By the parking lot,' I finished. 'I like working with you, Oyster Catcher. Can we get together again soon?'

'You send up a beacon in the chatrooms once a month and see if I answer. I'm going to be away for quite some time.'

'I understand,' I said, fully understanding.

Night had fallen. I had got off the bus that had taken me into the next state, and I was standing in front of the Institute of Science. I stood by the doorway, leafing through a textbook and watching a small male student in a multi-coloured baggy T-shirt. I read through the index, letting my finger wander down the page, as though I was looking up some important information. Another young student in a white labcoat hopped up the steps to the Institute of Science, and when I looked up from my textbook, the student held the door open for me. That was undoubtedly against the rules, but she did not seem to care. She would tomorrow, when the CCTV cameras showed her actions to the police.

I took the lift up to the sixth floor and got out. In my labcoat, jeans and long, blonde hair, I looked just like any other person there—a student or a technician. My badge was actually a receipt from the supermarket, beside a cheap photograph of me in the blonde wig, in the plastic covering I had taken off another student on a crowded bus several weeks beforehand.

I sauntered into the lab with my pen scribbling nonsense onto the paper of my clipboard. I reached over to a desk, took the reports off the desk, and walked out as I attached them to the clipboard. The scribbling continued as I stole a brief glance at the text on the papers.

I ran three storeys up, and did the same in the lab on that floor, then took the lift down to the second floor, performed my task there, then took the lift to the tenth floor, took some documents, then ran down to the seventh floor. Here the alarm was sounded as a means of evacuating the building immediately, to prevent any more documentation from being stolen. Thus all the lab doors locked themselves automatically, and I ran down the staircases alongside the other people in the building.

It would have been guessed that the data thief would be in the rushing crowd, but I kept my face lowered, looking at the stairs I was running down, knowing that all the cameras would see was a blonde woman with a labcoat.

I saw the door ahead and, together with a man of Chinese appearance, I ran through the doorway and out to the parking lot. The red Buick stood illuminated under a lamp, and I took off the labcoat and stuffed it under my thick sweatshirt. In all the rush and panic, no one saw that I had suddenly become very pregnant in a very short space of time. No doubt the CCTV cameras would have noticed, but it was going to take the police hours to trawl through hours of tape.

The Oyster Catcher was sitting in the passenger seat, and Jefferson sat behind the wheel. I threw the clipboard to the Oyster Catcher as I walked past the car, then ran to the fourth alleyway on the left. There I took off my sweatshirt, and took a box of matches from my pocket, stuffed them into a steel drum that I had placed there two hours previously, and set the sweatshirt, wig and labcoat on fire. I did not stay to watch the fire, but began to run, and I kept going for several miles. By then, it was pouring down, which I knew was going to happen. I had been watching the weather forecast for the last four days. The rain would put out the fire I had started in the steel drum.

So there I was, in my brown wig, jeans and T-shirt that was now translucent with the rain, standing in the street, alone. It was time to get my bag and leave. I would miss South Carolina.

I do miss South Carolina. I wish I was back there now.

'Tabitha,' Ben stood opposite me in front of my table. 'Are you all right?'

I looked at him.

'*Je le souhais.*'

Red and Blue

I sat on the settee that ran along the wall opposite the bar. Blue and red lights shone down from above, creating a purple haze around me. They say that, besides black, purple is the colour for death.

'Tabitha! Phone's for you.'

I ran to take the receiver from Ben. It was almost closing time, so he was busy behind the bar, even though it was a Tuesday night. The bar was full of students, lefties, crusties, wannabes and the disaffected. Over in the corner, Hepburn was strumming a duet with his friend Danny whilst people talked in quiet tones around the tables, creating a warm humming sound. A copy of *Socialist Worker* lay on the bar, having been discarded by several readers throughout the course of the day and the night.

'Tabitha, please, I need you!' The urgent voice at the other end of the phone was Kelly, an acquaintance from ten years ago. We had been introduced via a mutual friend in Blackpool, and now both of us lived in Stoke-on-Trent, and both had different names. Life is strange.

'What's up, Kelly?' I asked. Sometimes the platinum blonde did over react to her own shadow. Well, a lot of the time. She's a bit of a drama queen. I preferred not to mix with her.

'I'm in trouble. They're out there, I know they are.'

'Who?'

'I don't know,' Kelly whispered quickly, 'but I know they're going to get me.' She really did sound scared.

'I'll be there as soon as I can,' I said. We outcasts have to stick together.

I managed to get a lift to Kidsgrove with two of the regulars from the bar, and they dropped me off just by the car park in the centre of the small town.

From there, I ran up the hill away from the town centre, and to the lane that led to the Farmer's Arms and then the B-road. I made my way surreptitiously and steadily up the lane, staying close to the bushes that grew tall by the roadside, not wanting to be seen by anyone who might be lurking in the area to cause trouble for Kelly.

As I advanced, I became aware of people being there. I could not yet see them, but I knew they were there, lurking in the shrubbery. It's not a sixth sense—it's experience that told me. I decided the best way forward was the direct and obvious approach, so I put my best foot forward and walked up to the small wooden gate in a loud, proud and confident manner. I opened the gate and shut it noisily behind me, then strolled up the path to the small square bungalow that had been built on the farmland by the proprietor several years before.

The chain was take off the door to let me in, then frantically put back in place. Kelly was the tenant, as long as she didn't attract any kind of trouble. Farmer Braithwaite said that condition would have applied to anyone.

A transsexual living in Stoke-on-Trent would have an easier time if they lived in the middle of Hanley—the city centre—or in the student area, Shelton. However, Kelly, in her continuous search for peace, enjoyed living in rural areas, where she was exposed.

My head whipped back

As a palm slapped

My left cheekbone

I shook my head, trying to shake away the memory. I needed to focus on Kelly's situation. We heard the shouts recommence from outside the bungalow, and someone was trying the front door handle noisily, making an effort to be obvious. Kelly panicked and gave a small scream.

'Shut it,' I snapped. I had no patience for those who crumble under pressure.

'Get down on the floor behind the kitchen unit. If they break in, if they physically appear inside the house, shout "Red". You got that? Shout "Red".'

Kelly nodded to confirm she had taken in this instruction.

'I'll be back in a tick.' I proceeded to nip from room to room, not standing up at all, switching off all the lights, lest our shadows be seen, closing the curtains, making sure to avoid the windows. I did not want to be seen by the gathered masses, which is what twelve intruders added up to. I sneaked a peek out from a gap in the curtains and saw a youth in a blue tracksuit point to give orders, and another in a white tracksuit and baseball cap march past and disappear around the corner, in the direction of the kitchen. The others made their way round to the other side of the bungalow, towards the bedroom. I went to get the bedroom door key from Kelly. She sat underneath the table, her knees pulled up under her chin, and she had a sharp meat-cutting knife in her left hand, her dominant hand.

'What do you think you're doing with that?' I hissed, skidding to my knees.

With one sharp slap on Kelly's arm, the knife was knocked to the floor. 'Never use a weapon an assailant can turn on you.'

'I don't want to be—'

Kelly was about to break down in tears. I decided the only course of action I could take to prevent her wails was to be compassionate, but firm.

Quickly, I put an arm around the woman's shivering body and said, 'Just hold on for me, Kelly. Just keep it all in until it's over. I need the key to the bedroom.' Kelly took the key from her pocket and I went speedily to lock the bedroom door.

Kelly sniffed deeply, holding back the fear and trembling until the moment when I would give her permission to bring out her handkerchief.

In the kitchen, crouched under the table, I took hold of the knife that I had knocked to the floor, and, without making a sound, crept to what I correctly guessed was the cutlery drawer, which I opened, and took out all the knives and the solitary pair of scissors, which I wrapped in a tea towel, and placed behind the refrigerator.

I heard glass shatter and something fall to the floor with a tiny thump. The bedroom window had been negotiated. This put my brain into fourth gear.

Quick, quick. In the living room, I had seen a rickety old wooden chair.

Without asking, I turned the chair upside down and grabbed hold of the frame that held the legs together, I hit and hit the frame until the leg I had hold of came loose, and I wrenched it away from the frame. Now I was armed.

I crept back into the kitchen and sat under the table with Kelly.

'They've gathered around the back, so what we're gonna do is climb out of the living-room window,' said I, trying to convince Kelly that this would be the safest plan, when I wasn't too certain about it myself.

Kelly nodded and let out a small squeak.

Just as I had my hand on Kelly's shoulder to reassure her, a coated elbow smashed through the kitchen window, sending shards of glass everywhere, like an icicle thrown at a wall. Liquid ran down my forehead, and it was red.

'Red! Red!' Kelly screamed, a little too late, stating the obvious, drowning out the noise the youth outside was making as he tried to gain entrance through the kitchen door.

I slammed my hand over Kelly's mouth, holding the back of her head roughly, to keep the pressure against her lips.

Ow. Argh. Ow.

'Shtum,' I commanded as her eyes widened to tell me of the panic she felt in her stomach. The youth was shouting to his accomplices. The door was locked, so he needed the hammer to smash through the wooden door. A hammer would smash through bone, too.

'Are you going to trust me?'

Kelly nodded, but I kept my hands sweating over her mouth and skull.

Our silence was now mandatory.

'I want you to follow me in absolute silence. Have you got that? I mean absolute silence.'

Kelly nodded again.

'Take your heels off'—I had to be ruthless—'and your jewellery.' Kelly did as I bade and seemed semi-naked after doing so. Aware of the hammer hitting against the thick wood, and the hostile insults accompanying the action. I released my hands from Kelly's mouth and gave the final command: 'Now, follow me.'

I whizzed across the floor, skidding on my knees, and Kelly did the same, putting holes in the knees of her stockings. We reached the living-room carpet and crawled until I reached the window, whereupon I looked out into the secret night and saw that the coast was clear. The chair leg was tucked in the back of my trousers, and dug into the curve of my back as I moved. Cautiously, and in silence, I opened the window, out beyond its usual 45-degree angle, so that it was almost lying flat against the wall.

Kelly took my advice and put her stomach on the sill of the window and wriggled out, landing with a thump outside. I didn't even ask if she could've done it any quieter, because I knew she couldn't. I also went headfirst, but kicked my legs over my head, landing on my feet on the other side of the window. The chair leg dug into my back painfully and was almost knocked out of my trousers by the friction of the movement of my trousers and the curling up of my backbone.

'OK, are you OK?' I needed to make sure that Kelly had not injured herself, unaccustomed as she was to physical exertion mixed with terror. My companion nodded, so I continued, 'We're going to make a run for the road, heading for the main road. Have you got that?'

Again, Kelly confirmed her comprehension by nodding. She was beginning to look weary rather than petrified, which was probably no bad thing. At least when a person is petrified, their senses are sharpened by the rush of adrenaline. I didn't want a sleepy he-she on my hands when the wolves were out.

'OK, on the count of three?' I looked around hastily, and then, remaining crouched, I walked several small steps forward, flicking my head and my eyes everywhere, looking to ensure our safe passage to the road. Just as I was about to say, 'Three', I saw two faces bobbing in the bushes just by the gate that stood between the garden and the road. Plan foiled.

The back door splintered and a panel fell to the floor tiles. Yet more shouting and cursing as two men tried to knock through the kitchen door. *What to do next?* What to do next? What should we do next? *What next?*

Closing in, they were closing in.

I could not see daylight any longer.

I just saw them.

'OK, change of plan,' I said.

'What's the new plan?' Kelly asked, anxiously.

I wished I knew. And then I saw it, the beacon of hope and our future glory.

The ditch that ran alongside the bungalow. It was supposed to be a stream, but in summer, it dried up. (In winter, it occasionally flooded.) It would be muddy, but it would be safe, and would lead us the long way round to Farmer Jackson's house, where we could find refuge. *No.* Farmer Jackson would tell Farmer Braithwaite, of course.

Next plan, crawl along the ditch-stream until we came closer to Kidsgrove, where the pathetic stream meets the canal that runs just outside the main part of the town. That was the best plan. Now, to get to the ditch without being seen would be my next trick.

'OK, Kelly,' I whispered. 'Are you ready?'

'Ready for what'?

'OK, when I say "Go", run to the ditch over there, by those trees, and don't look back. We're going to that ditch over there.'

Kelly hesitated. I was sure she was considering the price of her skirt.

I crawled forward, looking in every direction, checking for a safe passage again.

I saw that there was no one else there on our side of the building, so I signalled with my hand and whispered, 'Go!' Kelly just ran to the ditch, running upright, and I ran, half-bent over, ready to dive down to the ground at any given moment.

Kelly landed in a wet patch in the ditch next to me. Ready for her to make a remark about this, I clamped my right hand over her mouth. She had made a grand effort at her jump down into the ditch. Suddenly, a part of me grew in estimation of Kelly. She was ready to do as I commanded. She obviously trusted me. Had I been too hard on her, just because we had such different personalities?

I knew I had a loathing for any bleached blonde in a short skirt.

We crouched in the ditch. I trained my eyes upward, looking for the intruders.

Kelly moaned next to me, 'You dress so dykey, so it doesn't matter to you. Do you know how much this skirt cost?'

The door slammed shut. Kelly was shivering. She was dripping watery mud on my rug, as was I. Going over to my wardrobe, I took out a set of royal-blue pyjamas and a large towel from the storage space above the clothes rail.

'Here.' I put the articles on the end of the bed. 'There's a bathroom down the hallway.'

'What am I going to do?' Kelly looked pathetic and helpless as she clung to herself tightly with cold, making her biceps bulge and stand out.

'Go and get washed,' I advised her. 'We'll sort everything else out in the morning.' I glanced at the blue rug, which was fast becoming purple-brown.

Kelly nodded and took the towel and pyjamas and left the room. I knelt to untie my laces, stripped completely, shivering and humming a tune quietly. As the tap ran to fill the sink in the corner of my room, I opened the window and tied the laces of my boots carefully to the catch of the window frame, and let the drying procedure commence. The remainder of my wet clothes was put into the pillow case that acted as my laundry bin, and I washed at the sink, letting my hair bathe gently in the upside-down world.

Wrapping my cold body in a towel, I rubbed my skin vigorously to feel some sort of heat. I wound a large towel around my head, twisting it until it had encompassed my dreadlocks. I put on navy-blue pyjamas and socks, then dug around in the suitcase under the bed to pull out a sleeping bag, which I folded over my left arm.

I tiptoed my way down the hallway, walking close to the wall. I tapped on the bathroom door.

'Kelly?'

'What?' the blonde whispered back.

'You sleep in my room. I'm going to sleep downstairs on a settee.'

There was no reply, so I tapped the door again.

'Kelly?'

'Yeah.'

So I entered the bathroom. Kelly was dressed in my pyjamas, appearing awkward.

'Can I stay?'

'Yeah. I'm giving you my room and jimjams for the night.'

'No,' she said slowly. 'Can I stay here?'

'You'll have to ask John, but we don't have any spare rooms, anyway,' I responded, glad that we had no vacancies.

'So what am I going to do?'

I was afraid Kelly would start wailing again, so I quickly asked, 'What do you mean?'

'I can't go back to Kidsgrove, can I?'

'You'll have to move on, then.' I shrugged. I had many times. It was no big deal.

'No way! I'm not letting them drive me out so that I have to start all over again somewhere else.'

'Well, that's nice and everything,' I said, 'but you're the one who nearly got their head kicked in tonight. I'm not going to protect you for eternity. You decide what to do. It's your life.'

The mask of fragility had been removed and her face grew dark.

'It's all right for you, isn't it?' Kelly spat. 'You, living here with a load of hippies! You don't have to live in the real world. I do!'

'I've had enough.' I turned my back to leave. 'Good night, Kelly.' The sleeping bag was heavy on my arm.

'That's right. Just walk away!'

'Good night, Kelly.' I left the door open as I descended the staircase, again staying close to the walls as I went.

The bar was black from the lack of light. I dragged the sleeping bag along the floor behind me, letting it brush against the table legs. The chairs were turned upside down on the tables, well balanced. I threw the sleeping bag up so that it would land in the settee in front of me. A pair of hands caught it. I sucked in air quickly, my fists poised at shoulder height in front of my chest.

'I was wondering when you'd come in.' It was Hepburn. He flicked his cigarette lighter and held it to the wick of a cream-coloured candle, which caught the small flame and began to glow brightly. Hepburn held the candle in a small earthenware tray and sat on the settee. I fell down to sit next to him, leaning on him for support.

'That's how it is,' Hepburn said. 'You take the power from the Source and you become full of that power.'

'Don't funny-talk me,' I mumbled. 'I'm not in the mood.'

'I know,' Hepburn put a loving arm around my waist. I always felt safe with him. The fact that I was not wearing any underwear was not an issue. 'You need perfect rest.'

'Mmmm.' The pain that I normally shoved to the back of my mind now burned in my throat, but I could not do anything about it.

'You did a good thing tonight.'

'Mmmm.'

'You're a good person. An important person. Don't you ever forget that,' Hepburn said. 'And besides, you're the only girl I know who's got balls.'

'Well you haven't seen Kelly naked, then, have you?'

We both laughed, and I fell asleep at some point. In that special place between consciousness and dreams, I felt Hepburn slowly let my head down to touch a cushion and cover my body with the unzipped sleeping bag. No matter what my dreams were about that night, everything was coloured red and blue.

Let it Be

I heard Hepburn's voice beside me, gently saying:

'Tabitha, it's me.'

My spine pulled my head up, and I tore up a crumpled tissue from my pocket and used the bits to wipe the snot and tears from my face. It was impolite and disgusting to let someone see that, even someone like Hepburn.

He sat beside me at the table, and I saw his eyes flick over the scrawlings on my notepad. I had been working on something new. My left hand pushed my dreadlocks back like a scythe through a jungle. I don't know if it was due to the subject matter of my writing or not, but thoughts about my life had taken over.

'What are you working on?' Hepburn asked me.

'Do you want to know?' I said.

'Would I ask if I didn't?'

I took a deep breath, then began:

'What if every piece of clothing you were wearing had a microchip inside it? It's not a Big Brother thing, but it's so that when you walk into a shop or supermarket, they will find out where you bought your clothes from, and therefore they can decide whether or not they want you in their shop.'

'It's sounds a bit sci-fi,' Hepburn frowned. 'More than a bit. And I think other people would find this story hard to swallow. I know I do.'

'I know.' I smiled in an awkward sort of way. 'I myself don't know what to think. Some people think it's already started, some don't, and some think it's a load of sci-fi rubbish,' I said. 'I don't know. Maybe it's all just scaremongering theory. It sounds mad, doesn't it? But for a spokesperson of a well-known supermarket chain to comment on it? I don't know.'

Hepburn picked up another point. 'But sometimes, the inconceivable is the actual,' he said.

I nodded. 'Life has taught me that the more outlandish something seems, the greater the element of truth there is about it.' I was thinking about my own situation in particular, as usual. I dropped the notepad onto the table with very little energy. My mind was taken up with other matters.

Hepburn waited for a moment, then asked, 'What's wrong?'

'I was remembering,' I told him. 'I started off remembering the good times, but then the bad times took over.'

I was aware that I didn't have a strong hold over the way I was speaking. It was difficult for me to focus in English when I was like this.

'Do you want to tell me about it?' Hepburn asked, as he moved his hand to comfort mine.

I looked down in horror and saw a tattooed arm coming towards mine.

My arms were held behind my back. He was whispering terrible things in my ear—perverse things.

The one in front of me was going to hurt me.

I stumbled backwards, and away from Hepburn, and perched on the edge of the stage. The whispering continued in my left ear. Hepburn followed me, faithful and kind, and sat beside me on the stage, with a substantial gap between us.

'What happened then?' he asked, looking at me. I hated it when he did that.

'I saw something bad,' I said, then became defensive and angry. 'I'm not telling you what.'

'OK,' he replied in a neutral tone. 'You don't have to tell me anything.'

'Good. I won't.'

'OK.'

Hepburn is a patient man. One of his 'fruits', whatever that means. I relented.

'I was remembering being in the Czech Republic four years ago, being with other outcasts. They were from everywhere—Europe, Africa. All exiles and outcasts. Persecuted. For some people, it was because of their ethnicity and for some people, it was their political beliefs. I find it *staggering* that people around here know so little about it—about what's going on.'

I laughed bitterly, then continued to talk about my memories.

'We all lived in this small village in the Czech Republic halfway between Brno and Zlín. It was tiny, in the countryside. It was nice. That's where I met my mate Marcus. He had been working in Sri Lanka and ended up with us. We were all happy, so happy just to be somewhere safe after leaving wherever we'd come from. All of us, outside the pub, grouped around two guitars singing "Let it Be". But we only knew the chorus—they didn't know the lyrics for the verses—so we kept singing the words "let it be" for ages. Quite fitting to our situation, really.'

I wasn't smiling. It was a good memory that burned my eyes, making them warm with sadness.

'We were all so *happy* just to be there.' I choked and began to cry. 'That's how it is when you first leave. You are relieved to be safe, and then later—for me it was five years—I began to miss where I'd come from.' I gave a faint laugh. I continued:

'Do you know, the first—maybe the only—thing I still miss was the street performers in the town centre.'

'Tell me about the street performers,' Hepburn said.

I inched closer to him, raising my body with my upper body strength, and moving sideways, and repeated this action until I was sat close to him, and smiled as I spoke:

'We'd all be out—in the summer—in the town centre. The mood would be good. Everyone out, chilling. The Bolivian band would be playing in the town centre. A disabled man would be playing his sax. It was fun. That's where I ran into Monique again. She had left Marseille a year before I had, because of, you know, trouble. I couldn't believe we were living in the same place again. It was incredible.'

'Keep talking,' Hepburn said, gently.

'I was remembering how happy we all were there,' I continued. 'We had all escaped, and were so glad to have made it. We could relax there—it was safe. You know, a small village where everyone knew us, and knew of us.' That was important to me. The people of the village had known of our backgrounds and wanted us to stay in their village. That had really touched me. I took a deep breath and went on:

'We were happy for a long time, and gradually, some of us became sad. It was because we missed where we used to live. We actually *missed* those hellholes. Even if we had loved where we came from, we would hate it because of what had happened. And we were sad because of the things that had happened.'

Tears began to fall from my eyes again, and I pushed them away with my fists.

'Now I'm here on my own.'

'Tabitha, you're not on your own,' Hepburn said.

'I am!' I replied. 'I'm the only one around here who's been through what I've been through.' I felt so alone, so different from other people. People here talked of dying for their cause, whatever that may be, but they didn't really know what they were talking about.

'Tabitha, you're not on your own,' Hepburn said. 'You've got friends all around you—you've got me. You're never alone.'

'But you don't know how I feel,' I protested. 'You have never had people after you for years. You've never had to leave one place you love and move to a completely foreign place because they have found you again, and you've never—' I stopped. I could not say it, so continued to explain:

'It's a barrier between me and everyone else. No matter how much you try to understand, you can't.'

'But isn't that the same for everyone?' Hepburn asked. 'I don't know what it's like to be you, just like you don't know what it's like to be me.'

I couldn't think of anything to the contrary because it was true. We all have unique lives, so how could anyone understand anyone fully? I should be grateful that I have someone, a friend in Hepburn, who is willing to try to understand as much as possible.

'Alright,' I said with another deep breath. 'Can I tell you about another memory that has made me sad?'

'Yes, of course.' Hepburn seemed prepared. He was always prepared.

'Two years ago, after I had left the Czech Republic, I was living in a safe house in a village west of Alcazar in the centre of Spain. It was a small village. I was staying in a safe house with two Romanies who had been driven out of Luxembourg, and one French woman. She had been an aid worker in China and had smuggled several girls out of the country so that they weren't killed. Annette. She was so *paranoid* all the time.' I looked down, then at Hepburn, and said, 'Like me.'

I cast my mind back to the past.

'It was summer, a local festival day, so we had prepared food for a banquet, and I had helped to decorate around the trees and the tables. We had carried the tables out into a nearby field. It was the one with the big beech tree in the middle. The sun was shining. I mean *really* shining. So nice.'

I stopped to wipe my face again. I sniffed and continued:

'We all piled into the field and took our places at the tables. They were long tables, with wonky legs, but they sufficed. Everyone from the village turned out. Alonso was still ringing the bell in the church tower when we all sat down to eat.'

'It sounds like a little piece of Heaven came down,' Hepburn said.

'It did. Then it became hell,' I said. 'We were all eating, laughing, then two coaches pulled up. Then they filed out. *Them.* They set out to destroy us. Tables were overturned, and people got hurt.'

'Tabitha, that's terrible,' Hepburn said.

'But I didn't try to save anyone!' I shouted. 'I could have, but I didn't.'

'You ran away?'

'No. It was weird. I just got fixated on—' I stopped and shook my head in disbelief. 'It's too weird.'

'No it isn't. Tell me,' Hepburn said.

'I needed to see the tattoos—the marks of being a—a—you know—one of them. I can't even stand saying the word!'

I wanted to say it, that word, to say what *they* were—are, but to say it would sound unbelievable and ridiculous. *Them*—I would never again be safe. I glanced at Hepburn, who was waiting, patiently, for me to continue, so I did.

'The serious ones carry certain tattoos,' I explained. 'They are found on certain specific parts of the body. I just grabbed hold of this one bloke and would not let go. He had no shirt on, and I was clinging to him, looking for those tattoos as he was overturning tables and trying to push me off him.'

'What happened?' Hepburn asked.

'I fought, they fought, everybody fought. It was a mess. We were surrounded. But there were too many of them.'

I shook my head, full of a frustration that dated back two years ago to a village in Spain.

'By the time I had stopped focussing on that one guy, it was too late.'

Now the tears flowed freely and I did not try to stop them. I was transfixed. I was there again, in that field, and as the scene played out again, I told Hepburn everything as it happened.

'He turned over the table, and Dr Emmaus didn't run fast enough. He was old, you see? He was hit in the leg with big splinters—the table had come apart and a sharp bit got stuck in his leg. The women had run back to the village.

'The men fought to protect the women. But Rocia was up in the beech tree. She was only seven, and she saw all that. It took us hours to get her to come down that evening.

'Yes, everything was overturned—the tables—the glass flew—the glass from the bowls. It went everywhere, but I was on the other side—from where everything had been thrown. I didn't get hit by the glass. It was all over the grass—shards of it gleaming in the sun. That was when I started to fight—when I saw the glass gleaming on the ground and heard the men yelling in pain. I still hear them sometimes. I grabbed hold of a glass jug and smashed it over a head, and then I got another jug, then a drinking glass, and threw that, and then another, and another. I went along the table, throwing glass. Do you know what damage that did? I do. I can still see it—what I did. And I hate it. But I had to do it.'

I was wiping my hands against my legs, trying to get rid of the feeling of holding the first glass jug I had used. I had to get rid of it. It was as though I was still holding it.

'You see, they didn't come all that way just for a fight. Not just a fight.
    'Ridiculous, ridiculous! Why would anyone go to those lengths of trying to get me?'

Ridiculous, but real. So very real.

'I kept on fighting. I kept fighting. I had to protect them, Dr Emmaus, Rico, Alonso, Sergio, Marco—the guys from the village. They had let me stay in their village—their *home*—knowing what they did about me. To fight and protect them was the least I could do.
    'So I was fighting, and I was fighting, and they realised that I was the one they had actually come for, and several of them surrounded me, and I got hurt.'

I couldn't say or even think beyond that. That's all the detail my mind could stand going into.

'And so I moved. I gradually made my way to England, staying here and there on the way.' I smiled, looking at Hepburn, glad that I had come to England, then said, 'But I can't forget what happened in the village in Spain. It felt so good, and safe. I thought I had security, for the first time in years. But no. I should have been able to save them.'

'Who?' Hepburn asked.

'The people in the village. I knew how to fight—really fight. And they all suffered because of me.'

In danger of emotion taking over, I got up and was about to run to my room, when I heard one of my names being called:

'Janey.'

I turned around. There was Mr Gladstone. He'd come for his property.

'Yeah, hold on,' I said, numb again. 'I'll go and get it.'

Mr Gladstone sat down at a table in the far corner. Hepburn went back to the kitchen, knowing that he could no longer reach me when I was in total denial mode—denial of anything. He was also aware that I appreciated privacy when dealing with Mr Gladstone. In his three-piece tweed suit and thick rimmed spectacles, he seemed somewhat out of place at O'Malley's. But I kept his secret.

I thundered up the stairs in my loosely-laced, knee-high, heavy boots, and went to my bedroom. I moved the wardrobe and took hold of the casing and its contents that were balanced on a two-inch-wide shelf that I had constructed there on the wall behind the old wardrobe with the purpose of hiding a valuable item— my laptop.

It wasn't the contraption itself that I found to be valuable, but the work that I did on it. The wardrobe was moved back into place and I emerged from the bedroom with the laptop over my shoulder in its bag, and I thundered back down the stairs and through the narrow hallway to O'Malley's.

'Here it is,' I said, as I crossed the room towards Mr Gladstone. I had to make up a story to cover Mr Gladstone and myself, so I said, in a voice loud enough for other people in the bistro to hear, 'It's been on the blink for weeks now. I'll kick off if I've lost any of my work.'

I placed the laptop into its bag on the table.

Mr Gladstone put down his broadsheet newspaper, and narrowed his eyes to look at me through those spectacles that were perched halfway down his nose. 'I'll see what I can do,' he said in his superior, plummy accent. Then he asked in a low voice, 'Is it clean?'

I nodded and whispered back, 'I wiped all the files and cleaned it of all fingerprints, and put the right barcode back on.'

'Good,' Mr Gladstone said. 'You'll get the new one in three hours' time. Go to St Clement's fruit and vegetable stall in the market. You will purchase some green bananas, sneeze and then go to the lift. Stay in the lift until you have the new laptop.'

I nodded, then asked, jerking my chin in the direction of the laptop, 'Who's the new owner of that going to be? I've been sending some pretty hefty emails to a couple of well dodgy types this morning. They're my sources, you see. And I got an email from Jean-Pierre, a guy I helped a while ago.'

'Ah yes,' Mr Gladstone said with recognition. 'The three Frogs that don't know how to croak.'

I looked at him because something suddenly made sense, and he added, 'How do you think they knew where to find you? I do hope they are doing well.'

'They are,' I said, flatly. 'I gave them a contact in Leeds, and they're being looked after. There's a certain Italian restaurant in the city centre with two French waiters and a Belgian cleaner.'

'The Powers That Be have been monitoring your emails,' Mr Gladstone told me. His forefinger tapped the laptop's casing, and he said, 'Rest assured, this baby is going to a deserving home. A small-time wide boy trying to make it big in the drugs trade. So we'll let him play with his new little toy, and let him wet his nappy when the police come knocking.'

'Two birds with one stone.' I smiled. 'I get in the clear, and the emails are traced to a drug dealer. Not bad, sir.'

'I know,' Mr Gladstone said. Then he picked up the laptop in his gloved hand, rolled up his newspaper and breezed out of the door.

For now, I was happy with that. A means to an end, but it felt like a cheese grater rubbing against my intestines because I knew it was wrong—to set someone up, despite what they did as a drugs dealer. I had too much on my mind, so for now, just like with my past, I would have to let it be.

La Raison d'Être

I arrived at the station, early as usual. On the train, I had managed to get almost two hours' worth of sleep. I had spent most of the night and the early hours of the morning typing up a report. I managed to send it to Jason just before 04:00. He had been emailing Jill for most of the night to keep her awake and amused on her shift, so he had only just gone to bed.

The ringtone of my mobile phone had woken me, and Marcus had told me that he wanted to meet me at the newsagent's shop inside Preston train station.

So there I was, stood by the glass newsagent's building, looking for the man who had been my first point of contact when I had arrived in the UK nine months ago. I dug my hands deep into the pockets of my camouflage trousers, apprehensive about meeting Marcus again. I remembered how laidback he was, but also how cold he could be, especially when there was work to be done. It was his way of coping with the stress. Like me. He was a good man.

I kept on turning on the spot, shooting my eyes at everyone in sight, ever alert, watching out for Marcus and any adversaries. My small rucksack was fastened close to my back against my sleeveless electric blue T-shirt, which showed how firm my arms and shoulders were.

Out of the corner of my eye, I saw a wheelchair. It approached from along the far end of Platform 3 and halted in front of me.

'Let's roll.'

I didn't look down, but walked at the side of the wheelchair, along Platform 4, and through the green wooden doors into the café. Marcus chose a table in the far corner. He lifted by the legs two chairs that got in his way, held them together in his left hand as his right hand made him spin, and placed them in a space by another table. I remained at the counter and ordered two orange juices and Danish rounds. I had remembered that Marcus didn't drink caffeine. He took better care of his body than I did. His body was a temple, as I remember. I had been wondering lately where that saying originates.

Looking over at Marcus now, it was hard to imagine that nine months ago, he had been a street fighter in Colombia, defending street children from the police who were sent to kill them. He was still muscular and trim, and dressed in his usual slashed jeans and black sleeveless T-shirt, with his head shaved down to the bone. But his skin, from his skull down to his torso, was decorated with blue, red and black. I wondered what had happened to him. A road accident? A fight where he had been severely outnumbered? I took the refreshments over to him.

'You're wondering why I'm not getting up to greet you,' Marcus said, with no intonation.

'Mind-reader,' I chanted, as if I was calling someone names in the playground.

'That's why I called you, girl,' Marcus started to explain. 'You are the only one I trust to do a good job, and the only one I don't like enough to get worried about.'

'You know how to impress a woman.' I sipped my orange drink.

'I don't get much practice,' Marcus replied, deadpan. He shrugged as he tore a circular strip from his sweet pastry, and went on, 'I've got fibromyalgia syndrome.'

'What's that when it's at home?'

'The quacks know sweet Fanny Adams, so they bung on this label that means sweet FA when it all boils down to it.'

He seemed relaxed, but chewed hard.

I bit into my Danish round. 'And the detailed version?'

With Marcus, there was always the FA version, and then an explanation broken down into smaller leagues. He leaned forward with intent.

'Two years ago, I get these pains in my legs and back, ranging from dull aches to stabbing, ceaseless pain that would not go away. And I was done in, every waking hour.'

'I remember,' I acknowledged, thinking of Marcus nine months ago, lying asleep in the back of the van. The rest of us were on edge, twitching nervously as we were being driven inland from Weymouth, where we had arrived on a ferry.

'My symptoms progressed to severe headaches, pain all over my body, ranging from the dull aches to the stabbing pain, and nausea. The pain in my legs is almost unbearable, and the muscles are often weak. That's why I use this thing these days.' He stroked the arms of his wheelchair with bitterness.

'So this fibromy-wotsit is responsible?'

'That's what the neurologist says, but the illness itself is a complete mystery,' Marcus said. 'Virologists say it's caused by a virus, immunologists reckon it's to do with the immune system, psychiatrists say it's a psychiatric disorder. Do you get the picture? All these theories are really nice and everything—'

'But it doesn't help you,' I finished for him. Marcus nodded.

'No one's sure where it comes from or how to treat it. Different things work for different people, but we don't know much more than that.'

Marcus leaned forward and said, 'Homegirl, my heart stops beating in the middle of the night sometimes. I jolt awake, gasping for breath.'

'So your body has learnt to work around it,' I mused. 'Is there anything I can do?'

'You're wondering why I got you out of bed,' Marcus said, one hundred percent correct.

I took the straw from my glass and just drank mouthfuls. I had missed breakfast to get here on time. It's not as if I didn't care about his condition, because I did, but I wondered why he had summoned me here this morning.

'I've had Aruna researching the whole fibromyalgia thing, and she's pulled up some pretty interesting stuff.' Marcus reached behind his back and thrust forward a clear plastic bag containing pages of information. He put the bag on the table and said, 'I've brought the highlights.'

I took the wad of paper from the bag and ran my eyes over the text, which I estimated was size 8 and which covered both sides of the paper.

'*Depression is a possible cause,*' I read, then looked up at Marcus. 'Well, that would be a possibility for you.' I continued reading, and read out, '*The suppressed guilt theory.* Again, that would be a possibility for you. You know, everything from your past.'

Marcus looked at me sharply. 'You think I don't know that?'

'Sorry,' I said, scanning the subheadings again, not feeling any sense of shame or anything.

'*The sweetener theory*,' I continued reading out loud. That caught my attention with a jolt in my stomach. Where had I heard of that before? I had heard of it before.

'It's all to do with the chemical in some sugar replicants. Sweeteners.'

'I know what replicants are,' I said, without looking up. I was engrossed with what I was reading under this subheading.

Marcus talked of his knowledge of this food sweetener:

'It's said that if you ingest enough of the stuff, you'll develop symptoms as though you have MS, you know?'

'Multiple sclerosis,' I said. 'The nasty one.'

'Exactomonto,' Marcus said. 'And look at what products it's used in.'

I looked in horror at the list of products—products that were purchased by most food consumers in the western world.

'But how can they get away with it?' I asked.

'Get this,' Marcus said, pulling out the sixth page and pointing to a highlighted name. I was taken aback.

'So they would never condemn its use!'

'Correct,' Marcus said. 'But you need to consume quite a lot of this sweetener per day to build up the toxins which would cause the symptoms to develop.'

'But is it possible for a person to consume enough if their diet is unhealthy enough?' I wondered out loud.

'Girl, it's more than possible,' Marcus said. 'It's been said to be the cause of MS in quite a number of people. They stop using this sweetener and their MS seems to be "reversed", which is impossible, as you can guess, with "real" cases of MS.'

'So it can be like the illness never existed?'

'Correct,' Marcus nodded. 'But think of how much Caucasians tend to sweeten their food. Maybe the best thing to do is not to stop using this sweetener entirely, but to rotate its use with other sweeteners, so one month you use Sweetener A, the next month you use Sweetener B, and so on. That way the chemicals won't build up in your system.' He chewed the centre of his Danish round.

'Forgive me for being nosey, but what exactly is my role in this crusade against the Dark Side?'

If it was merely information-gathering, Aruna was more than capable, as I well remembered from how she had 'helped' me when I came to live in England nine months ago.

'The institutions listed and underlined in the text—' Marcus began.

'You want me to sweep them?' Of course. What else?

'Now who's the mind-reader?' Marcus said. 'Yes, I want you to sweep them. They have the answers for the questions these pages ask. Get whatever you can.'

'And you are offering—?'

'See the last page,' Marcus said.

I did, and my heart missed a beat. I raised my eyes to look at my new employer. 'I'll need a team of, say, five. I'll work alone with the other five as base contacts in the relevant national states.'

'I imagined so.' Marcus had a knowing smile that was annoying. He knew the way I worked: alone, just as he had. We didn't trust anyone else enough to do the job with us. 'Which is why the fee is so big,' Marcus continued, and washed down the last of his pastry with a swig of orange. 'It's to split between you and your team.'

'Where does the money come from?' I asked. I did not normally ask that question, but I knew that when Marcus had 'worked', he did it for the cause, not for the money, which was the other reason why he was often alone. Most of the time, he had been without an employer.

'You don't seem to get this,' Marcus said. 'This is a growing worldwide problem. There are international leaders who have loved ones suffering, and they want answers, hence the money is in place. They don't have the, er, "diplomacy" skills that you have.'

Marcus looked at me, then leaned his arms on the table, rested his head on them, and looked up at me from the tabletop, with a glint in his eye. 'You've never been curious about the source of wealth before. Why now?'

'It's a lot of money,' I said in the hope that Marcus would guess what I meant, because I didn't want to say it.

Marcus squinted at me, and asked, 'Are *you* in it for the money?'

'I've *never* been in it for the money,' I said, hotly. 'I wouldn't know what to do with the money.'

'Cha right!' Marcus had to put down his juice before he spilt it, and laughed. 'So what do you do with it all, girl? I know you ain't got no swimming pool or Mercedes.'

'I invest it wisely,' I said, not wanting to divulge my private business.

'How wisely?'

'South American schools wisely. Indian colleges wisely. What's it to you?' This was private.

Marcus sat back in his wheelchair, grinning, and said, 'Just checking your heart is beating.'

I wondered if he sat back in his chair because my words made him pleased, or had he thought I might hurt him?

'They say that something about you is changing.'

'Like what?' I knew exactly what.

'They reckon you're still playing this game but you don't know why any more.'

'They're talking out of their backsides,' I retorted, a little too harshly. 'I should've guessed. They always fart out of their mouths.'

'In the beginning it was all about your own survival,' Marcus said. 'And it grew from there. Is that what it's still about? What makes you do the things you do?'

'Leave it,' I said, in a tone that could not be compromised. But I knew the answer myself. Without a home, living outside of society, I had only known one way of life. The least I could do was to make sure that as few people as possible knew what it was like to be me.

'How is your fan club at the moment?'

That made me angry. Anything that made me think of them when I hadn't already been thinking about them made me angry.

'As loyal as ever to their cause,' I said, trying to laugh, but my throat made a weird sort of choking noise instead.

'Always laughing, ain't you, girl?' Marcus leaned forward again. 'That's how it is, isn't it? How it is with most of us, but then you start to feel it, don't you. You're feeling it, ain't you? You can't pretend to yourself no more, can you?'

'I'm off.' I rose. 'I've got work to do.'

'Grabbing the money to run?'

'See you in two weeks' time,' I said, trying to ignore the way his verbal scalpel was dissecting a small part of the front lobe of my brain.

'Coventry station, by the news stand,' Marcus confirmed. He grabbed my hand. 'Girl, I stopped running.' He gave a short, bitter laugh, then said, 'Hadn't you better?'

I snatched my hand away, and stalked off, wiping away the memory that his hand had left on mine. It felt disgusting and painful, but that wasn't Marcus' fault. It was nothing to do with him.

As soon as I arrived home at O'Malley's, I ran straight up the stairs and into my room. I threw my bag down onto the bed, and reached underneath the basin of the sink to retrieve the key that had been secured there with sticky tape. Then, rummaging in the bottom of the wardrobe, I found the screwdriver. I sat on the window sill and reached up to unscrew a panel behind the curtain rail. This then fell into my hands, and allowed me to reach into the gap and take hold of the money box inside. I chucked the box onto the bed, opened it with the key, took out six bundles of notes, then dialled a number on my mobile phone.

'Hi, Mr Gladstone—Yes, I'll need access to another phone for thirty minutes—Three hours' time—I'll be on the 16:24 to Manchester Piccadilly—At Crewe? I'll be in coach B—Yes—No, it's OK—Thanks.'

So it was agreed. Mr Gladstone would sit opposite me in Coach B and put down his mobile phone, which I would then take and use in the buffet car. The phone would then be returned to Mr Gladstone in Piccadilly station on the escalators, and finally would be passed on to a 'deserving cause'.

I took the six bundles and locked the box and put it back where it belonged. Mr Gladstone would take half of one, and the other half of that bundle would go to Helena, who would deal with the other five bundles. Over the space of a week, Helena would gradually put the money into bank accounts for Monique, Jefferson, Dieter, Rick and Annette. They were my 'team'. I had met Dieter and Rick in Belgium, whilst wandering for several years around Europe. Dieter constantly made fun of my inadequate ability to speak German, but he was sharp, and easy to work with, alongside all the mockery. They would work separately in their own countries to obtain the information required. The hits would have to be simultaneous so that the alarm would not be raised before the other hits were made. This would be especially tricky because of the time zone differences. Some of the team would have to obtain the information whilst the various institutions were in operation. But it was do-able, as I had proved in the past.

My route to the train station took me on a short cut through the back streets, near where one of the canals passed. The cemetery was in front of me, across the busy road. I was concentrating on the traffic too much to notice the two men approaching me.

'Gissya bag,' the taller one commanded.

'Tie a knot,' I replied, still looking at the traffic so that I could cross the road.

'Gissit!' he said again, and flicked open a knife in his left hand. So I knew he was left-handed. I just looked at him.

'I can't be bothered today. Go away.'

The shorter man made a grab for my bag, so I made a grab for his arm, and stood aside, letting the momentum pull him forward into the wall of the house behind me. Then I put my left arm around his stomach and pulled him to the ground, and landed on my back next to him. A quick elbow in the stomach and he was gasping for breath as his friend came towards me with the knife. I hate knives.

I hooked my foot around the back of his knee quickly, and he hit the tarmac. I scrambled on top of him, and quickly punched him on the right side of his face, and grabbed hold of his left wrist to knock the knife out of his grip. He began struggling, so I kept hold of his left hand as I punched his face again twice. The knife fell out of his hand. I punched him again.

'Never do that again,' I said, calmly, and got up, taking the knife with me as I crossed the road, and dumped it in a rubbish bin where it belonged. I didn't think twice about anything. I had a train to catch. That was my reason for existing today.

The Die is Cast

I woke up in an unfamiliar bed to the beeping of the alarm clock on my mobile phone. 08:30. I got up, replaced the pillows to how they were when I arrived, and pulled the sheet and blankets up to the headboard, smoothing them out, ready for the next person. I had an overwhelming urge to thank someone for this bed, but I did not know who to thank.

I put on my clothes, splashed some water on my face in the bathroom, and took my rucksack with the only belongings I possessed—a writing pad, a spare set of clothes and a sleeping bag—and went down to the kitchen where Jonas Gladstone was sat at the pine table in his three-piece grey silk suit with a sky-blue tie. His assistant, Aruna, handed me a plateful of an English breakfast. I sat down with Mr Gladstone.

'I trust that everything is well with you?'

I decided to lie. It was the polite thing to do.

'Yes, thank you,' I said. I did not want to show much gratitude or any humility. This man was merely a function—a cog in a machine.

'Aruna has found you somewhere,' Mr Gladstone went on. 'A man by the name of John Spencer. He runs a student bistro or something along those lines. He takes in all sorts of waifs and strays, and he has a room going spare.'

'How much a week?' The breakfast was good.

'Thirty pounds.'

'Is that all?' I was surprised. That was an incredibly cheap price for *any* rent, let alone for a landlord knowingly renting a room to someone like me, judging by what I remembered from when I lived in Blackpool in the early nineties.

'Stoke-on-Trent *is* cheap living,' Mr Gladstone said. 'The economic boom of the eighties seems to have completely bypassed the city. But you are expected to do work in the bistro and help with the upkeep of the rooms.'

'So I won't be the only lodger?' The thought of sharing space and the possibility of having my life exposed were not exactly appealing. I didn't *have* to talk about anything with anyone, and I was very guarded about everything I said to anyone. But things have a nasty way of coming out.

'Relax,' Mr Gladstone said. 'John Spencer tends to take in stowaways, doesn't he, Aruna?'

Aruna smiled at me shyly, then went back to typing on her laptop.

I could guess by this woman's black and green *salwar kameez* that Aruna was not her real name. That tended to be a Hindi name, which did not fit in with her clothes. Maybe she was mixed race? I wondered what her story was, then I told myself off.

It was none of my business.

Mr Gladstone reached into his briefcase, and pulled out several passports and two bus passes, and held them out, saying, 'These will come in useful in Stoke. Don't bother getting a car. The buses are good enough.' He put the documents and wallets down in front of me and said, 'Ann Scargill, Tabitha Meera, Tina Black and Jane Rushmore.'

Then he took two cards from his jacket's inside pocket.

'John Spencer's address at O'Malley's in the Hanley area of Stoke-on-Trent, and my business card. Oh and—' He reached further into his briefcase and handed me another card:

'This is your first contact for a job.'

'What sort of a "job"?' I asked with suspicion.

'Information gathering that does *not* involve breaking into government laboratories.' Mr Gladstone stared into my eyes with a hard stare.

'The die is cast, then.' I shrugged my shoulders, and took the card from his fingers.

Thus began my journey. Aruna took me to the bus station and waited until my coach had left, and then she went on her way. I did not know the destination of the coach. All I knew was that I was to get off the coach when it reached its final destination, which was not going to be Stoke-on-Trent. Not yet. As the coach made its way along the motorway, I saw signs for Portsmouth and Chichester. My limited knowledge of the geography of England told me that the coach was heading east, along the south of England. I did not question this because, at the time, I did not know where Stoke-on-Trent was situated. With my mind at relative ease, I caught up on my sleep.

The coach arrived in a large car park next to a bus station. I disembarked with my rucksack and stood by the side of the coach, wondering what would happen next. I didn't have to wait long, because almost immediately, a striking-looking young woman with long blonde hair approached me.

'Are you a friend of Mr Gladstone?'

'What's the right answer?' I asked. I did not know who this person was.

'I think that was the right answer,' she replied with a smile. 'Come on.'

I followed her out from the bus station, and onto the street, which was swarming with people on this hot July day.

We passed a mother pushing a pushchair. The blonde infant was dressed in sickly girlish pink and was licking an icecream, getting it all over her face. I thought that she deserved to look a mess. I decided I should find out a bit more about this blonde woman who was leading me through the crowded streets. We seemed to be in some sort of seaside resort, but it seemed much trendier than what you would think of when you think of English seaside resorts. There were no knotted handkerchiefs in sight.

'So who are you?' I asked, without much politeness.

'Helena,' she replied. 'And you are—?'

'Let me see.' I slid one shoulder strap of the rucksack off my shoulder and took one of the passports from the front pocket.

'I am—' I fumbled for the last page with the identity, nationality and date of birth typed on.

'I am Tabitha Meera,' I said, grimacing at the passport photo of myself. Aruna had taken that photo just before I had fallen asleep after arriving at Mr Gladstone's house. No wonder I looked so rough in the photograph. I put the passport back into the rucksack. It said I was Irish. That might go a little way to excusing my mixed-up accent to others.

'Where are we going?' I asked Helena. 'I thought I was to go to Stoke-on-Trent.'

'Yeah, you'll get there in time,' Helena waved the importance of my journey away with a hand.

'What do you mean I'll "get there in time"?' I was new to all this organised network stuff.

Helena looked back to talk to me and almost bumped into an older man, so she said, 'We'll talk when we've stopped walking, OK.'

'OK,' I agreed. We were walking at a rapid pace. It was best to talk about 'stuff' when we were more sedentary.

Helena stopped outside of a fast-food outlet.

'Are you hungry?' she asked.

I was about to protest at the prospect of eating at a fast-food restaurant, but the truth was I was hungry. It was almost three o'clock in the afternoon now. The weather was hot and I hadn't had a drink since breakfast time.

'Yes,' I said.

'Right, I'll take you to a little café I know,' Helena replied. 'It's a little bit more intimate there.'

'Whatever,' I said, shrugging.

'This way, then.' Helena walked off cheerfully ahead of me, and I jostled my rucksack into place again and followed after her. I noticed that Helena dressed in a way that craved attention. The pastel colours she wore—a denim skirt and baby pink T-shirt—stood out brilliantly on her tanned skin, so they were eye-catching to begin with. The clothes drew attention from several men because they were all tight-fitting, the skirt's hem reached only a few inches below her bottom, and the V-neck of her T-shirt went about as low as a V-neck could go. For a friend of Mr Gladstone's, she certainly went out of her way to attract attention.

We reached the café several minutes later, and I sat at a table in a shaded corner by the back wall. That way, I could see everyone who came into the café, and assess my ability to render them unconscious, if the need arose. Helena approved of my choice of table.

'Good. We're away from prying ears,' she said. I thought the phrase was 'prying eyes', but then I thought that Helena would not mind eyes prying. Tart.

'I'm hungry,' I said, with meaning.

'Of course,' Helena said. 'How silly of me.'

She flicked her hair as she turned to another table and took the menus and placed one in front of me, and held on to the other herself. She looked over to me and said, 'I can recommend the stilton and cranberry baguette.'

'I'll go with what I know,' I said. 'Ham and cheese.'

Helena went up to the counter to order the food and presumed what drink I would want, which wasn't really a big deal. I concentrated on each person who was coming in and going out of the door, as well as the ones going to the toilets, the small children running around, and the people passing by the window. I never felt exhausted with this constant vigilance. It had been a part of my life now longer than I could remember.

Helena sat down, and took a small circular casing from her handbag and flicked it open. It was a mirror and miniature make-up kit. She busied herself for a few moments with applying more make-up to her already shiny face, and then flicked it closed, just as the baguettes arrived. The waiter smiled at Helena and walked away, looking back over his shoulder. She flicked her hair again, and began to eat. I picked up the baguette with a loathing for this bitch. Weren't we supposed to be here with a purpose? So why was she acting like this? She was attracting far too much attention for my liking.

'How far is Stoke-on-Trent from here?' I asked, hoping to get some sense from the skin display with blonde hair.

'Oh, a few hours' drive away,' she said, as if she didn't really care.

'Not wanting to be rude or anything,' I said, 'but when are we going to get there?'

'Oh, don't worry,' she laughed. 'You'll get there tonight. Just relax. Enjoy yourself!'

A small part of my stomach was seething at this point. The woman did not seem to realise how much her carefree attitude was annoying me.

'I *had* planned on getting there before the Fall,' I said.

'We will,' she laughed.

I wasn't *that* funny.

Helena made attempts at small-talk, commenting on the café's décor and the weather, and she made an attempt to bring me up to speed with current events in the UK. All I gave as a response was either a 'hmmm' or a monosyllabic murmur. I found it strange that a young woman with her apparent attitude didn't comment on any of the men who looked at her with intent. I was hungry, I was thirsty, I was in England, I was annoyed.

We finished our baguettes and paid the curly-haired, Mediterranean-looking man who was behind the counter. I put the change back into the front pocket of my grey combat trousers, and the man smiled at Helena, she smiled back, and then Helena and I went back out onto the street. I hoped that all the smiling that was going on between Helena and other people in the street was just a flirting thing, and nothing more. Inflicting pain on Helena was not something I wanted to do particularly.

As we stood on the street corner, Helena's right hand scrambled around in her handbag for something. All I wanted to do was to go to Stoke-on-Trent, wherever it was. Helena zipped up her handbag, and took hold of my right hand. I thought she was going to pass something to me—a map, a name, or something else that might be of some help to me. Instead, she said, 'We could do something for a while, if you like. We have time.'

This was unexpected. So was my response.

I squeezed her hand, smiling, then with my left hand picked her up by her stomach, and ran down the alleyway with her over my shoulder. The top of my rucksack grazed her forehead. Oh dear. I dropped Helena and pushed her against the wall, pinning her with my right knee digging into her stomach, and my right hand at her throat.

'Now, tell me who you are and what you are doing, and make it real.'

'Helena, my name's Helena,' she said, with tears in her eyes. 'I work for Mr Gladstone. I do, really! I was just trying it on. Please!'

I pulled her up off the ground so that I could look straight into her eyes. She was telling the truth.

'You stupid bitch,' I said. 'You should know that someone like me doesn't go with *any*one.'

Helena nodded furiously, making small squeaking noises as she did. I put her down on the ground, and picked up her handbag, and gave it back to her.

'So, how do we get to Stoke-on-Trent from here?' I asked.

Helena sniffed, trying to compose herself again, pulling her skirt into place. It was probably the first time she'd pulled the hem down from her bum deliberately. Miaow, saucer of milk for Tabitha.

Helena stumbled over her words: 'I'll take you to the train station, and then when you reach London Victoria, you go to London Euston, and then get the northbound train to Stafford. At Stafford, you change and take the train to Stoke-on-Trent. If you get to Manchester, you've gone too far.'

'So take me to the station,' I said. Helena made her way past me nervously, flicked her make-up case open again, trying to cover up the scratches on her forehead.

I was relieved to get on the train and get away from her. Stupid blonde. It's people like me who suffer because of people like her. She flirts, and people like me get hurt. Sometimes, I really hate women. They know nothing about real life, and they don't want to know.

The train journey did not go without event. The train was packed full of people, and some of us were standing in the gangways. Myself and several middle-aged women were stood with our suitcases outside the toilet of our carriage. I couldn't hold it in any longer, and went to use the toilet, leaving my rucksack outside. If anyone touched it, I'd have them.

Not having used one of those toilets before, I was not accustomed to the proper usage of the buttons. I managed to '*pssssht*' open the door with the 'Open' button, then closed the door '*pssssht*' with the 'Close' button, and sat on the seat and used the toilet. As I was about to get up, I saw the door to the toilet sliding closed, then open again, and then closed. I looked at the panel by the door, and there was an illuminated button that had the word 'Lock' written underneath it.

I decided that since everyone had seen everything by now, I would just get on with it, so I stood up and pulled up my combats, washed my hands, '*pussssht*' closed the toilet door, and stood opposite it, guarding my rucksack. No one dared to look at me, which made me smile. It was the first time in months.

I sat with my head on my knees under the heavy blue blankets, wiping the sweat from my forehead with the slack of the blanket closest to my body. Unable to hold it in any more, I let it out. The wails were loud. I was astounded at how loud they actually were.

My bedroom door was opened and a familiar voice spoke, patiently, but with firmness: 'Tabitha, it's me.'

My bed sank in the bottom right corner with the weight of Hepburn, and I became silent, and pushed the blanket back. I could never let my emotions out when other people were around. I had to pretend. Knowing Hepburn was making me different, but that made me angry with myself. I couldn't let my guard down. I shouldn't let my guard down. Two of my dreadlocks marred my view of Hepburn, whose hair hung down onto his T-shirt.

'It's not even six o'clock,' he said.

'I didn't mean to.' I couldn't say 'sorry'. That would be weak, and I already felt weak for crying. But I had to. It was normal for someone who had been through what I had been through. But who else was there who had been through the same as me and was still alive?

'I was going to do some work,' I said. My eyes focussed on my right knee, which was covered by my blue woollen pyjama bottoms. Despite the summer heat, my skin was covered from my neck down with a T-shirt under my pyjama top, and the trousers came down to my ankles. That seemed sufficient to me.

'I was going to make an early start.'

'So what happened?' He pushed his hair back and tied it in a ponytail with the red band that was around his wrist.

'I woke up,' I began, 'and then my mind just shot back to when I came to England nine months ago, and I woke up in one of Mr Gladstone's houses. The one in Devon. It was as if I was back there again.'

'A flashback,' Hepburn nodded. 'That's what it's called—a flashback.'

'I have these "flashbacks" all the time,' I told him. 'About *stuff*.'

'I thought so.' Hepburn thought for a moment.

'I want them to stop,' I said. 'But the strange thing is, most of the time, they don't bother me. I'm *that* used to it. I mean, yesterday, I was reading the newspaper, and I heard them shouting—in my head—and I just kept on reading the newspaper. Is that *normal?*'

'You are normal for a person who's been through what you've been through.' Hepburn echoed my thoughts. 'They will stop in time. When your brain has remembered all it needs to remember, and when you've dealt with everything your mind needs to deal with—'

'But that could be months!' I wasn't happy about this.

'More like years,' Hepburn told me. 'Be ready for the long haul. This sort of thing doesn't just go away after a couple of months, or even a couple of years. It's going to take years for you to be all right.'

'Great,' I said, not at all happy with Hepburn saying this. But I knew it was true.

'Tabitha, I'm your friend, and I'm only going to tell you the truth,' Hepburn replied. 'And being truthful, this has been going on for years already, hasn't it?'

I waited for several moments to pass while I thought, and remembered how my mind had been remembering for the last three years. Maybe it was more than three years? I didn't know.

'It's been rough, hasn't it?' Hepburn said with knowing.

I nodded. 'It's been years since I first heard the voices of memories.'

'Do you see the pictures, too?' Hepburn asked. 'Do you get memories like that?'

'Yes,' I replied with disdain. 'And I can feel memories.'

'How do you mean?'

'When I'm alone, watching TV,' I said, 'I can feel them. When I'm in the kitchen making tea, I can feel them. I don't want to talk about that.'

'That's OK,' Hepburn said, reassuringly. 'You don't have to talk about anything you don't want to.'

'But I do want to,' I said, 'to get rid of the memories and the feelings, or I might explode.'

'So what stops you?' Hepburn asked.

'I don't know,' I said. 'Maybe it will hurt me. Maybe I won't be believed.'

'I believe you,' Hepburn said.

'I know,' I replied. 'But to me, when I start thinking about it, it all seems so far-fetched that I don't believe it myself, but I know it really happened.'

'It did really happen,' Hepburn said with certainty. 'I know it did.'

I wanted to ask him how he could be so certain. There was something very definite about his certainty. It came from somewhere. I often thought that Hepburn had some sort of insight into people and sometimes their lives, and it's strange, but I think it came from his beliefs. All he ever said was that he was grateful for being 'fruitful', whatever that means.

I began to cry again. This time, I was quieter, and more controlled. Of course I was. I wasn't alone. I wanted Hepburn to leave me alone. The words that went through my head were, 'I want to be alone to grieve'. But no one I knew well had died, so why did those words keep going through my head? They had been going through my head a lot lately.

Hepburn then asked, 'What were you crying about?'

I shrugged.

'Tell me or I can't help you,' he said, plainly.

I hesitated, then said, 'I want it all to stop. I wonder when it will stop.' I reached behind my back for a pillow, and as I knelt, I hit it on the bed and against the wall several times, and wailed through gritted teeth in frustration.

'Tabitha, you're not the only person in this house, you know?'

'I'll try to be quiet,' I said, then the pain struck me again. 'That's what they want—for me to keep quiet. To never talk about it or them or anything.'

'I don't think you're ready to talk about it yet,' Hepburn said in a gentle tone. 'But can you tell me about how the flashback affected you?'

'Why do I hate women so much?' I asked him.

'You hate women?' he repeated.

'I know it sounds stupid because I'm a woman,' I said. 'But I do—sometimes I really hate women.'

'Can you elaborate?' Hepburn was clearly lost on this.

'They are so pretty and wear pretty clothes and have happy lives and they don't know anything,' I said quickly. This had been building up inside of me for a long time. It was something I really believed.

'And how did you come to that conclusion?' Hepburn asked, puzzled, but not frowning.

'I see them all the time,' I said, knowing this sounded ridiculous, like everything else I wanted to say, but I kept going: 'I see them on the bus with their make-up on, and their skintight clothes and they are always smiling. They don't know anything.'

'All you are seeing is the masks that people wear,' Hepburn said. 'Those women may be miserable, but they don't want the people on the bus to know that. The women you see on the bus may have been through all sorts of terrible things. Don't judge a book by its cover.' This was said in a kind, gentle way. Hepburn had a way of telling me off without making me feel horrendous.

'I want it to stop,' I said. 'I want to have a life again. To not be looking over my shoulder all the time in case *they* find me again. I want to be able to vote. I want to be able to have a proper bank account. I want normality.'

I couldn't believe I had said that. Normality. But normality is boring. I'd rather kill myself than be normal. Being normal *would* kill me.

'I think I know what needs to stop,' Hepburn said, carefully. 'Your way of life needs to stop. The way you live and work needs to change. You shouldn't feel that you need to live like that.'

'What *choice* do I have?'

Hepburn continued with a hand on mine: 'You can't help what made you run—you can't help the fact you were persecuted.'

'Shut up,' I commanded, and pushed him slightly.

'No I won't,' he said, and carried on: 'You *chose* to do the things you do—and with the right motives —but it's got you stuck in a dark place, and compounding the damage already done to you when you were persecuted.'

'I said'—I pushed him harder—'shut up!'

Hepburn grabbed a hold of my wrists, knowing what I could do to him, and pulled my body towards his, and he held me as we sat side by side facing opposite walls on my bed.

'Listen'—Hepburn spoke against my cheek—'when something is kept a secret, power is held over you, but when you make that secret known to even one person, the power held over you that binds you up, is broken.'

'You mean the people who persecuted me?' I was confused.

'In part, yes,' Hepburn said. 'But what I really meant was the powers of darkness. They have a hold over you because you keep what happened to you a secret, but also your way of life is very secretive, and that's not good for the soul.'

'I know,' I said, 'but I don't know why it makes me feel like this.'

'We were made to be relational,' Hepburn explained. 'You know, to live in strong community with other people.'

'Like we do?' I was starting to understand some of what Hepburn had been telling me since I had moved to O'Malley's.

'Yes,' he said. 'And anything that separates us from other people can only be a bad thing. Harmful to us.'

We sat in silence for several moments, until I spoke again: 'I don't know when the next time will be.' My body convulsed forward as the sadness took hold again.

Hepburn held me across my shoulders, warm and pure.

'The next time for what?' he asked.

'When *they* will find me.' I couldn't speak for a while until I had composed myself again. 'Will it be today, being kidnapped in the street? Will it be a brick through the window next week? When will it happen again?'

Hepburn breathed and held me tight.

'Oh, Tabitha,' he said. 'You need more than *any* one can give you.'

And that made me cry.

Choice

Hepburn was about to go on stage, and I had been looking forward to his performance all day. However, now, darkness had filled my mind with

screaming. I couldn't stop screaming.

It was the process, the routine, the drill. We all knew it by heart—me, us and them. They went out with the sole purpose of tracking us down, sometimes to kill, sometimes to injure, and we—I—knew it would happen. Every day I left the house, I knew that I might never come back. There was no way I could stop it. They knew where I lived, and they were intent on coming after me especially. Everyone said I had suffered more than the others.

With me, it was more frequent and more severe. They were after me in particular. Why me? Was it because I was not afraid? Was it because I held everyone else together? And we could not go to the authorities, because we knew what their reaction would have been. Out of all of us, I was the strongest, holding everyone else together. Everyone else had to take amphetamines to cope. I chose not to. I didn't want to go there.

Jenna was standing at John's side behind the bar, and Aristotle was sitting on the stage, dressed in red, with the right half of his hair sprayed red. He wore a black trainer on his left foot, and a red one on the other, and he was absent-mindedly throwing three red apples into the air, catching them in a continuous stream in his left hand, and then throwing them up again with speed and no hesitation, making a circle of red in the air above his left shoulder. Juggling took his mind off his problems, temporarily. He was like me—stuck in the past. Aristotle, or Jim, as he was known when he wasn't juggling, was a gentle man. Too gentle to stop his wife from battering him. Juggling took his mind off his scars—the ones in his mind as well as the one on his leg. To Aristotle's left, Hepburn was stood, preparing.

Hepburn pulled the red bobble out of his hair and, with the bobble on his wrist, smoothed back his hair, clasped it into a ponytail shape and wound the bobble around it again. He was at ease, waiting for the next four minutes to pass till he was to go up onto the stage with Danny. Hepburn glanced over to the bar, checking on Danny's state. Danny had a glass of whisky in his hand. He was nervous. He always was when he was about to play, but Hepburn kept an eye out for him, and had, on occasions, taken Danny away from the bar, as he had been too drunk to belch. Hepburn was always looking out for other people.

I was hot and bothered. My mind was becoming more clouded as I wanted Hepburn to help me more and more, but I did not want to trouble him. He was busy, and anyway, he was too good to hear my problems. Nice people should not hear what I have to say.

Arrghh, that didn't hurt, yeah right,

come on then, come on

Arrrghhhhhh.

Things were going round and round in my head and wouldn't stop. O'Malley's was in darkness except for the candles on the tables, and the coloured lights that shone haphazardly from the ceiling. Even seeing my two long-haired friends, Danny and Hepburn, getting up onto the stage with their guitars didn't distract me from how I was feeling. Sometimes nothing works. It was too dark for me. I didn't like being in the dark when other people were there. Sometimes nothing works. Being in the dark made me think too much, too fast, too paranoid. I felt sick, and the heat was getting to me too much, so I took a walk.

It was late, and I was strolling through Cobridge, a notorious danger area, but it was where I felt most at ease. I passed the flats, the young men who hung around the taxi drivers, standing by their vehicles, talking. The litter flapped in the wind as it tumbled along the street, driven by the breeze. This was a poorer area, inhabited mainly by the ethnic minorities. I could be in any English city.

I walked this route most nights these days. Concentrating on other things helped to filter things from my mind. So most people in this area were used to seeing me walking around here.

One street, another street, it was all the same. Everything was always the same. Faces changed, places changed, but everything carried on the same. Even despite everything I did, there would still be people living in poverty all around the world, people dying of illness, people dealing, people wheeling. When was all the suffering going to stop? When was everything going to be made better? When would it all be clean?

Maybe what I did didn't make an impact in the real world at all? And even if it did, what was the point? We live and we die, or that's the theory. What is the point of anything? I was walking back up Hope Street, when I saw a familiar figure on the street corner. Gemma. In her short red skirt and tight white T-shirt, she looked almost six stone.

An improvement. She had stopped injecting into her arms months ago, due to the veins collapsing, so now she injected into her toes. These were on show in cheap, strappy high heels, but men tended to not look at a woman's feet before handing over ten pounds, or five pounds in the case of females who insisted on using condoms.

Diane and Suzanne, two middle-aged mothers, came around the corner and joined Gemma, chatting and preparing themselves mentally for their next client. I had spent many an afternoon having cups of coffee with these women, paying for them to eat something, even just a sandwich, as the crack strangled their feelings of hunger, and the heroin smothered thoughts.

Sometimes, on a Friday night, I hung out with them at the church that loomed over the edge of the red-light district. It was warm there, and we could get a cup of coffee.

I did not blame Diane, Suzanne, Gemma or the fourteen-year-old called Adele for doing what they did. They didn't think they had a choice. It's all they had ever known from childhood, but at least on the streets they got paid for it.

And the crack and heroin? I can understand that, too. In their own way, they were doing the same as the average reveller on a Friday night—getting off their faces to escape their problems.

The only difference was that they were constantly getting off their faces to escape their problems via addictive substances, and so they needed to work more to fund their drug habit, and the vicious circle continued.

The crack made them stay awake longer, but was even more addictive than the heroin, and made their lives more chaotic than heroin did.

Heroin. A funny name for a drug. But to me, each of these women and girls was a heroine, a survivor. And they kept looking for a way out, to leave their problems behind completely, and they would try to escape—really try—but then the withdrawal symptoms would augment and highlight their own incredibly low self-esteem. Then they would meet an acquaintance with a bag of heroin, and they would be back to square one.

But I believe that every attempt to break free is worth it, and is one more step along the road to freedom. There's all sorts of heroines in this world.

A voice drew me from out of my thoughts:

'Oi, Tabitha.'

I looked round and saw a teenage boy, leaning against the railings that protected the music shop, and I glared at him.

He spoke again: 'Fritz sent this.' He pushed a note into my hand as he walked away, up towards the town centre. I walked up to the top of the bank, and standing under the rainbow in the doorway of the lesbian pub, I read the note:

> Toilets, the shopping centre, unseen by anyone, including the CCTV cameras. Thursday 12th, 10:00.

I knew of Fritz. A Danish expatriate who had sought refuge in the UK during the Second World War. The locals and the authorities thought he was German, and so he had been arrested and spent most of the following years in prison, plotting revenge on everyone and everything. I had met him on two previous occasions and didn't like him, but that didn't stop me from wondering what he wanted.

To get across town without being seen by anyone, including the CCTV cameras. I had done this before in London, Seville, Marseille and Leipzig. I knew what to do.

No one looked twice at the elderly Asian woman, a widow with a white cardigan wrapped around her white *salwar kameez* with a white headscarf, bent almost double, leaning on her stick.

Her eyes were downcast, concentrating on where her feet would go with each step. She was making a courageous attempt to reach the main glass doors of the shopping centre.

Heavy, fast breathing.

I had been running.

My legs hurt from running so far.

Some people pushed, some people stood aside for me.

I had started in Shelton, at the train station. I had gone in to the station dressed as I normally did, with my blue rucksack. The women's toilets served as my changing room. Off came the trainers and combats, and on went the thick black tights and *salwar*. Off went the T-shirt and on went the *kameez*. This was a good time to use the train station toilets as a dressing room. The commuters had all taken their train to work, and it was too early for the average day-tripper to be up and about. So I had the mirror to myself, and no bizarre looks from other toilet users. Still, I had my 'I'm a Theatre Studies student' speech ready, just in case.

In the mirror, I applied the latex layers to my face, sticking them firmly into place with the specialist skin glue I used from time to time, giving the appearance of wrinkled flesh. Foundation make-up, much darker than my usual skin tone, was put to use, as was the dark wig that had been fashioned into a long plait. On went the headscarf and flat white sandals that I had recently found in a second-hand shop. They looked a bit worn. I put on the finishing touches, and then put the remainder of the make-up in a carrier bag, and stuffed my clothes into the rucksack.

I would pick that up later from the ticket office, stating that my granddaughter had left it earlier by mistake. The carrier bag of make-up was left on the bus that took me from the train station to the town centre. I would claim that from the left luggage department at the bus station later this afternoon, when I would be dressed in my T-shirt and combats.

I made my way through the crowd of denim short skirts with pink T-shirts, and the long stripy T-shirts with the denim trousers. There was a queue for the lift. I could have taken the escalators, but a woman of my frailty was better suited to taking the lift.

Up to the second floor, and I got out, helped by a young woman in a knee-length denim skirt with a small boy in a blue and green striped T-shirt, and a pushchair. This family headed towards the toilets, only to be turned away by a woman in a cleaner's tabard with 'out of order' signs at her feet and a mop in her hands.

The young mother and her brood came back towards me to get the lift back down to a lower floor, and the mother smiled at me, probably under the impression that I didn't speak good enough English to understand 'out of order', so she didn't bother trying to tell me.

The cleaner looked at me as I approached. She could not see my face, so she said, 'Hello, the toilets are out of order.'

Then, slowly, in a slightly raised voice, waving her hands to convey a negative:

'No toilet. Do you understand?'

I looked up, and she saw my dark, lined face and brown contact lenses, and I said, in my best Bengali accent, 'I have a colostomy bag, you little Hitler. Do *you* understand?'

'A colostomy bag?' She repeated, loud enough for the teenage gang who were stood by the top of the escalator to hear. 'You'll have to be quick, then.'

I took more doddering steps as the woman in the tabard held the door open for me. After I had shuffled through, I heard it close securely.

'Congratulations.'

Fritz was leaning against a sink. I moved towards the large Dane.

'Whatever.' I stood up straight, no longer frail. 'What's the deal?'

'Jumping the gun, little dog. Always jumping the gun.'

Fritz could be annoying. He had been annoying on both the occasions I had met him in the past. He had figured out one or two things about me, and liked to poke fun. Fritz had a master plan for his existence, which was basically to agitate as many people as possible. He was also a very perceptive person, who had enough people in his pocket to be able to obtain information on almost anyone he chose. He had run into a brick wall when he had tried to obtain information about me. No one knew anything. This had led Fritz to draw conclusions. And they were close to being correct.

'Cut to the chase,' I said. I didn't want to entertain Fritz's company any longer than necessary. I didn't know where the advantage in power lay: with me or Fritz?

He was the man with the height and muscles like balloons; he had several hangers-on and had guessed some aspects of my life. I was the tall female who was in demand.

This was a difficult power struggle. I gripped the walking stick with my right hand.

'Who's eager?' His eyebrows moved up and down.

I had one hand compressing Fritz's windpipe before I could blink. I let go of his throat, and Fritz pushed me away, coughing. Several of his entourage had moved towards me, but Fritz waved them away. When he had finished coughing, he looked up.

'Did I touch a sore spot?' He grinned.

'You could have sore spot*sss*.' I emphasised the '*sss*'. I raised the walking stick horizontally in the air as a show of my ability and willingness to fight him.

'Why all this?' I asked. 'Why all this disguising and getting-here-without-being-seen palaver? It was easy enough, don't get me wrong. But why?'

'Because we have a job, and we want the best,' Fritz said. 'And you are among the best.'

Flattery always works.

'Why, thank you,' I spat, lowering the stick to stand it at my side again. 'What's the job?'

He handed me a piece of paper, which I unfolded and read. I saw the financial figure at the end. It made no difference to me.

'Why?' I asked, pushing the paper back into his hands.

'Does there need to be a reason?'

'Forget it,' I said, and started to walk away.

Two of Fritz's disciples moved to the door to block my exit.

'You can't walk away from me that easily,' Fritz said, with a slight laugh. I didn't let people get away with laughing at me. Even if it took years, I always had the last laugh. I had an accurate and long memory, unfortunately.

'Fritz, I've walked away from bigger people than you,' I said in a condescending tone. Fritz was a child compared to some people I had met. I had made my decision, and I was going to tell Fritz in no uncertain terms. 'I'm exercising my right to vote, and I choose to vote with my legs. I'm out of here.'

I took further steps to the door, walking with purpose. I could make those clowns at the door fall, no problem.

'I know about you and your choices,' Fritz said, in a mocking tone. That was not a good sign. And then he said it:

'A choice of any man in uniform.'

I spun and hit Fritz on his temple with the walking stick, as though I was teeing off on a golf course.

I had never *chosen* that, and Fritz knew it. Fritz knew too much. And I saw the blood running, bubbling at the surface of his epidermis like a spring coming up from muddy soil.

I swung the walking stick round as I spun, kicking out backwards at the follower of Fritz who had tried to make a grab for me. The stick hit Fritz in the stomach, as I had anticipated, and he fell to the ground. It all happened so quickly that the entourage could do very little to stop it, even if they had had the courage to try.

Fritz fell to his knees, and I kicked up at him, and he fell back. It hurt my toes in the open sandals, but that did not hinder further action. I brought the stick down on his stomach, and then stood away from his writhing, breathless body, silently threatening everyone else, turning on the spot.

'So you all want to take me on? All of you?' I looked around at the faces. Some seemed nervous, some didn't know me. I went on with my declaration, still turning on the spot with the stick upright in my hand as though it was a crowbar.

'I'm leaving. This is my choice, and this is the last we'll ever hear of each other.'

'Why?' Fritz mimicked me. I watched him get to his feet, holding his stomach and lower ribs. The blood still flowed from his temple. He had stood away from me, which is why he didn't bother me.

I turned and walked right up to him, close to his face, and said, 'The only jobs I ever did were the ones that stopped people getting done. It's not exactly the sort of thing you want doing. I'm not up for that.' I shrugged. 'Anyway, as of now, I'm retired.'

Several of Fritz's fools started to laugh.

'That's right,' I said with more conviction this time and a sincere grin. 'I might have a time relaxing, on state benefits.'

'You'll get bored,' Fritz sneered, and directed his next comment at his followers: 'They always do. Look at Marcus.'

'Bored people are boring people.' I shrugged. 'Now, I'm leaving and this will be the end of it.'

'Don't worry,' Fritz said. 'Nobody is irreplaceable. We'll find a replacement for you. That won't be a problem.'

I scrunched up my face and shoulders in false, gushing gratitude. 'You make me feel so special.'

Pushing the door open without much force, I hobbled through, leaning on my stick, keeping my face turned down to the ground. The guard in the cleaner's tabard asked, 'Everything sorted?'

'It will be,' I muttered, without looking up.

I shuffled over to the lift, and as I went to the basement and took a place at an ornate white circular table, I thought about what I had done and where my choice would take me. What was I without my 'work'? Would I get bored?

Flashing Lights

Get away.

Stop it. Stop it.

No. Stop it.   No. No.

The club was in semi-darkness. It was just after twelve o'clock in the afternoon and the usual Wednesday group were in—an anarchistic meeting who used us a base address.

They were OK as people, I suppose, but they're like the far right in a way; they don't believe that far right extremists have the right to speak in this so-called free speech society, or even the right to live. That's where I disagree with the far left. All people have the right to exist and speak, no matter how ridiculous and terrible their beliefs.

I was lying on a settee near the bar, with a desk lamp leaning over my shoulder, helping me to read. But I was having difficulty in concentrating. Thoughts of the job I had completed for Marcus plagued my mind, as well as the other stuff.

'Tabitha, phone's for you,' Hepburn shouted out from the kitchen.

He kept the receiver in his hand until I picked up the phone receiver in the hallway and called back, 'Got it, ta.' Then I heard the click as Hepburn went back to chopping up a lettuce, and asked, 'Who is it?'

'Three guesses.'

I feigned a middle-class accent: 'I'm sorry, but I've got no idea who you are.'

'You're kidding me,' said the American.

'Sure am, Oyster Catcher,' I replied in my normal voice. 'Long time no see.'

'Yeah, that's just what I was thinking,' replied the Oyster Catcher. 'Well, I'm in England for a couple of days, and I thought I'd see you if you weren't busy.'

'Not particularly,' I responded. I could finish off the research I was doing for a local authority at the weekend. 'So, where are you?'

'Blackpool,' the Oyster Catcher said. 'Weather's not bad.'

'Why don't I come up and meet you there? I've not been to a funfair for ages.'

'OK, yeah, meet you behind the airplane ride at twenty-one hundred hours,' said the Oyster Catcher. 'Is that OK for you?'

'Yeah, that's cool for me,' I said. 'See you then, and stay stoosh.'

'You too.'

The phone went dead.

Now to get organised. A bit of money. Make sure my mobile's charged up. Yep, it's fine. Right, now to find my train pass.

I got into Blackpool North at 18:36, so I had time to kill. I made my way under the familiar subway and up, out onto the main street, which was packed with people who had just come off the train, or people who were going out on the tiles, even though it was a Wednesday evening.

I strode down the familiar streets, and made my way quickly through the town centre, hoping that I would not recognise anyone, or be recognised.

Of course, I had changed much since I had last been in this place. My hair was now shoulder-length and dreadlocked, I had lost weight and even my face had been changed.

It had been over ten years since I came here to live, to escape. All I had found was the same hassle, so I had left and wandered around mainland Europe with no hope for several years.

Things had changed when I had met the Oyster Catcher. We met in Krakow, funnily enough, and worked and travelled together until our work in South Carolina had put a temporary end to our partnership.

I decided to take a walk down the promenade, as the weather was warm, the sky was pure blue and the atmosphere was pleasant enough at this hour.

Shop names had come and gone, but the content had remained the same over the years. Candy floss, candy rock and 'novelty goods', which were basically sex toys.

I decided to take a walk on the other side of the street, near the sea, where there were fewer people, and those people tended to be couples, holding hands and strolling romantically in the late afternoon sun.

So, there I was, standing behind the airplane ride at the funfair under a darkening sky, which was lit up with all sorts of unnatural lights. A row of coloured bulbs flashed blue, green, red, yellow, blue, green, as I walked to the left towards the main exit and entrance of the park.

I had an uneasy feeling.

Although I was surrounded by people out for a good time, I had the peculiar knowledge that familiar faces were here, in the fairground, looking for me.

'There you are!'

I stopped and spun around.

'Catcher, you're looking, er—'

I would have loved to say, 'well', but the truth was, he looked 'weary'.

'I am,' he replied, with a slight smile. He was trying to put on a brave face about something.

'Catcher, why are you here?'

'To see you, of course.'

'No, why are you back in Britain? You said hell would be hosting ice skating contests before you came back here.' I recounted the phrase from the past.

The Oyster Catcher lit up a cigarette, then said, 'I don't remember, do you smoke?'

'Only when I'm set on fire,' I replied, shrugging.

'That's not funny!' the Oyster Catcher shouted at me.

'Wasn't trying to be,' I muttered.

'Let's get walking.' The Oyster Catcher looped his arm through mine, and began to walk at speed towards the exit. He wasn't smiling. 'I don't think we're safe here.'

'You get that feeling, too?'

'Why? Do you?'

'Something feels so familiar,' I said. 'I think they are here.'

'Aww shoot!'

'Why are you here?' I asked again more fervently, not wanting to know the answer.

'Two months ago, I landed in Klatovy in the Czech Republic,' the Oyster Catcher said. 'And they were there. Must have seen me in the town centre or something. I wasn't lying low 'cause I didn't think I had to. So, after being followed home one night, I just upped and left in the middle of the night, and went to Regensburg, Germany.'

'Let me guess, they were there?'

'How did you know?' A brief comedy moment.

'Lucky guess.' I looked at him. 'Come on, this is me you're talking to.'

The Oyster Catcher acknowledged this fact with a nod, and continued: 'So, again, I packed my bag and went. I got to Augsburg and then to Mannheim, Dijon, Rennes, Rouen. Each time, they were there. I think they've been hacking into my bank's systems to find out where I am. That's the only explanation.' He shrugged and went on, 'I've not emailed anyone, texted anyone or—'

'But you phoned *me!*'

The Oyster Catcher and I stood stock still, facing each other. Realisation dawned on us.

'They're all around us,' the Oyster Catcher said, his face white.

'I can feel them.' Tears sprang to my eyes.

'Look around,' the Oyster Catcher said. 'What can you see that we can use?'

'Bumper cars, roller coasters, open storeroom door.'

'Let's go,' the Oyster Catcher said, and he put his arm around my shoulders, as a man would to his girlfriend, and we hoped we looked calm and casual and normal as we made an extreme effort to quell the panic that was rising in us.

The storeroom was dark, apart from the coloured lights flashing in through the windows. The rectangular room held a copious amount of opened cardboard boxes, full of leaflets.

We walked through, having closed the door behind us, and we kept walking, looking for a place to hide. A staircase stood at the end of the long room, and so, with no alternative, we climbed it quickly.

And heard the storeroom door slam shut on the floor beneath us.

Where to hide?

Where to hide?

Where to hide?

Where to hide?

We came to a small room of laundry skips, full of dirty linen sheets from the hotel—and a door at the far end.

'Quick, get into one,' the Oyster Catcher whispered.

'Wait,' I replied, and carried on to the door, and looked back to see the Oyster Catcher getting into one of the laundry skips on the side of the room by the windows.

I opened the door and saw a room with absolutely nothing in it, so I slammed the door loudly, then hurried to get into a skip and cover myself with gravy-stained linen.

Footsteps. Lots of them. From underneath the tablecloths, I could hear them breathing, shuffling their feet, existing.

'Right,' said an aggressive Scouser. 'We saw them two doilems come into this place, and they're not downstairs, so where the hell are they?'

'Why not check these boxes?' It was a northern French voice.

'Don't pass "Go" and don't collect two hundred pounds,' the Scouse man spat in ridicule. 'It's a bit obvious, innit? Do you really think they would make the job so chuffin easy for us? Well, do you?'

I heard him, the Liverpudlian ringleader, overturn the skip next to me in a violent, forceful manner.

My stomach felt as though two pairs of hands had grabbed hold of it, and my skull prickled as sweat broke out. A hand swept down and grabbed some of the top layers of my hiding place, and the footsteps went back the way they had come.

At least ten minutes passed before:

'Hey?'

'Yeah, I'm still respiring,' I said, sitting up, perspiring from my skull, back and groin. As I looked around me, I saw that my right trouser leg had been exposed, possibly when some of the top sheets had been taken.

'Ready?' The Oyster Catcher jumped out from his skip, looked back at the stained bedsheets amongst which he had hidden, and shuddered. I climbed out from under my tablecloth and became nostalgic.

'Remember that garbage dumpster in Red Wall, San Francisco?'

'Now, that was gross!' the Oyster Catcher agreed.

'Let's go.' I led the way to the room of nothingness, and we went down the staircase and came to a heavy wooden door that had been our way in. It took several hefty shoves for us to push it open, but we did it, and took the direction of the main exit again.

There were so many people. I could not see the Oyster Catcher. He had completely vanished from my sight. I ran. They were running after me. I could feel them.

I came to a bus shelter, full of people—old women mostly. There were two gay men there, who looked at me, knowingly. One winked and took my arm. The taller of the two looked into my eyes and I understood. I crouched down, my back against the shelter wall, and my body hidden by the two men's legs. The tall man looked down, with a finger to his lips. I closed my eyes with my head tucked under my arms.

I realised suddenly that the air was colder. I opened my eyes and looked up. I was alone in the dark bus shelter.

My stomach was gripped again as a silhouette of a man in a suit appeared at the opposite end of the shelter, and shone a torch on my face

Blue...Blue...Blue...Blue...BlueFlashingLights...Blue...

I awoke, comfortable and swaddled in blue. Hepburn sat at the end of my bed, his hair hung over his face from either side like deep brown curtains that were trying to shut out the light that emanated constantly from his face. He was smiling in a concerned way.

'Catcher?' I looked around. He was not here. Where was he? Did he get hurt? Where was he?

Hepburn put his reassuring hands up in the air.

'Calm down, calm down,' he said. 'The Oyster Catcher's fine.'

'So where is he?'

'Last seen heading towards Manchester Airport,' Hepburn told me. 'He's thinking of spending some time with a friend in India.'

'So he's not hurt?' I asked, intently.

'No,' Hepburn said. 'But you should concentrate on your own injuries at bit more.'

I looked down. I pulled the duvet up to my shoulders, to the shoulders of my black T-shirt.

'You were lucky those two guys had the guts to come back,' Hepburn said.

'Yeah. I'm really lucky,' I said, not opening my mouth too wide for fear of the four cuts on my lips splitting open.

'When is it all going to stop?' Hepburn sighed.

Tears rolled down my face. 'I need it. I need it.'

'You need five men to hold you down, beat you and rip your clothes off you?'

'I need the buzz,' I wailed, blood running down my chin. 'It makes me know I'm alive. I'm sick, I know, I *know!*'

I looked at Hepburn, the one person I had trusted implicitly in thirteen years.

'Can I tell you about my dreams?' I grasped hold of the duvet, feeling pain in my arms as I did so.

Hepburn gazed at me with such kindness. I can't describe it.

'I've been wanting to hear about them for a while now,' he said.

'OK. OK,' I breathed slowly. This wasn't going to be nice. 'OK, there's the one where I'm in the school that's sort of a concentration camp.'

'Go on,' Hepburn said.

'We were all stood in a line, and the teacher, she went along the line asking us questions. Then she would take some of us out to another room, where we would be "punished".' I felt my eyes growing wider with pain. 'There were other people there, who hit us with canes, hard. Then things carry on as normal—'

'What do you mean?'

'The same things happen again and again. It's normal,' I said with a shrug, still gripping the duvet.

'Then what happens?'

'That's the bit I don't like,' I went on. 'We were in a van, all of us, being taken somewhere on the motorway. I was planning ways to escape, but I didn't. Just like in real life.'

Hepburn leaned forward.

'Why is that just like real life?'

'Because I never escaped. I always wanted to, but they've kept coming after me, even here.' I burst into tears again, resplitting the cuts around my lips. The blood dripped onto the duvet cover.

Hepburn took some tissue paper from his pocket and handed it to me, to hold to my lips.

'Do you want to tell me about the others?'

'Yes.' I drew breath. This was not easy. 'There's the town, where I live at the top of a block of flats, and I know *they* are watching me on CCTV, and they can find where I am because of where the lift in the flats goes. I go to work or to the shops, then I try to outwit them when I return at night. They do not try to harm me—only watch me. But I don't want them to know where I am.'

'So what happens?'

'I try to climb the staircase, and there's people stood there, watching me. But no, I know that *they* know I am there, doing that. So I try to climb up the lift shaft. But no, it's so futile. And that's the end of that dream.'

'It's a very paranoid dream,' Hepburn said.

'I think I have every right to be paranoid,' I shot back with more sarcasm than I had imagined I could throw at him. I drew breath again.

'The next one. Where I'm in an underground government bunker,' I said. 'I keep walking along a corridor, then when I get to the end, I go down the stepladders to the next level down. All you can see is blackness and blue lights on the filing cabinets. I keep on walking and going down to deeper levels, then this man starts walking behind me.'

I saw Hepburn twitch but pretend to be unaffected. I carried on.

'He makes me go with him down the levels, but he doesn't hurt me. I just have to go with him. We go down the ladders, and every time, I hurt my back. You know? That bit of my back that's really sensitive.'

Hepburn nodded. Once, he had touched that part of my back, and had experienced my reaction. I had not hurt him too badly.

'It hurts every time we go down a ladder. There's a man standing there at the bottom of the ladder, looking forward onto the corridor. I see him and the man behind me sees him, but he doesn't do anything. Why? Who was he? Who was the man at the bottom of the ladder? Was he a witness? Who was he? Why was he watching? Who was he?'

I felt the tears welling up in my eyes again, and Hepburn saw, so he stopped me.

'It's OK,' he said. 'You don't need to know yet. Just keep talking. Are there any more dreams like this?'

'Oh yes,' I said, with a bitter laugh. 'It's gross. It's the worst. If I don't tell you now, I might never tell anyone ever.'

'OK.' Hepburn held out his hands and I clasped them tightly. He said:

'Go for it, in your own time.'

'I'm lying on the floor, and I'm paralysed. I try to scream, but my jaw gets paralysed open. I can't move, and there's black oblongs moving all around me. I try to scream, but I can't. I just see these black oblongs, and there's one in front of me, standing over me. The others have moved away. No prizes for guessing what that's about.'

I started to laugh. Hepburn looked our hands. I kept on laughing and laughing until

'Noooooooo!'

I was scrunched up again, my back against the headboard of the bed, and my body pulled up around me. I clutched my head, feeling my dreadlocks, an unintended symbol of suffering people, and that spurred my tears on.

I felt Hepburn's arms around me. I breathed in from his neck. He smelt safe.

'Tabitha,' he said. 'I'm going to send you somewhere. Somewhere where no one will ever find you.'

'Yeah right.'

'Will you believe me?'

Hepburn had never lied to me before.

'Yes.'

'It's a place where you can be safe. You can change there. Do you want that?'

'Of course I do.'

'No, I mean, do you *really* want that?' Hepburn asked in a firm tone. 'Not because I want it, but *you* have to really want it.'

'Yes.' I couldn't look up, even though I felt a touch of hope and was trying to hold on to that.

'Then it stops *now*. You'll leave tomorrow and when you get there, you will start your new life. And you will start to use your own name. Tell me again, what's your real name?'

'Danica.'

'And what does that mean?' Hepburn asked.

'Morning Star,' I droned. It meant nothing to me. Why couldn't I have a normal name? A name that meant something, instead of being given this weird, communist name by parents I could hardly remember?

'The most famous and influential person who ever walked the planet was called the New Morning Star,' Hepburn said. 'It was because he chucked out the old and brought in new beginnings for people. *You* can have a new beginning.' He re-emphasised this point.

'Who was he?' I asked. There was some reason why Hepburn was telling me this. It always seemed as though he wanted to tell me something, but did not think I was ready to hear it all yet.

'Just get some rest,' Hepburn said, getting up. 'You've got a long journey tomorrow.'

'Where are you sending me?' I asked.

'To a life-changing place. It changed my life,' he answered. He blew me a kiss and left me alone to contemplate. Blood was still running from my lips as I fell into a concussion-induced sleep. In the darkness of my mind, letters appeared in flashing lights:

D A N I C A

Day is Breaking

Winter had come and gone, as had the worst of my feelings.

The sun shone in through the open window, accompanied by a gentle spring breeze. I was aware of a change that had taken place in me over the nine months I had been here. It felt like a change for the better.

The familiar sound of the lilt in Hepburn's voice and his most recent song filled the air as I busied myself in tidying the room I shared with three other women. I took the tissues, hardened from my tears of the night before, from out of my yellow bedsheets and threw them in the rubbish bin by the door. The others had let me have the bed by the window, which held a glorious view of the grounds, and beyond that, the civilian street.

I found it amazing how the abbey had lasted whilst the city had been built up around it. Of course, the abbey had had repair work carried out on it over the years. However, the building contractors had done their utmost to restore the seventeenth-century abbey as close as possible to its original form, and it had survived the test of time.

Unanswered letters lay strewn on my yellow bedsheets, as well as a folder full of those to which I had responded. My roommates Claire, Felicitas and Marie-Yvette were studying with *Sœur* Hélène, the oldest sister here, so I had the room to myself. Therefore, I had seized upon the chance to take the box of paper from under my bed and begin to get it in order.

There was a knock at the door. It was *Sœur* Camilla.

'I heard you cry last night. Are you all right?'

'Yeah, come in,' I replied, gesturing for the Jamaican lady to enter.

'Music from England?'

'He's a friend,' I said. 'He's the one who wrote me all these letters.' I pointed to a pile of paper on my pillow. 'It's strange to hear someone singing in English after living here for so long. I miss him.'

'He must be a good friend. And he is a talented singer,' *Sœur* Camilla observed.

We had arranged several days ago for *Sœur* Camilla to help me to fix the top parts of my hair that had grown in the last month. *Sœur* Camilla pulled the chair from under the desk by my bed, and thumped it down in the middle of the room with a force that made me cringe.

'Sorry,' she said, looking at me with a knowing apology. 'I do your hair now?' *Sœur* Camilla asked in her third language. We could both speak English, but *Sœur* Camilla wanted to practise her French, even though she had lived here for four years.

'Yeah.' I sat down, and *Sœur* Camilla took out a tub of beeswax from her gown, and gently took hold of a dreadlock that rested on my left shoulder and began to twist the hair at the top firmly.

Sœur Camilla was thirty-five years of age, and her dreadlocks touched the base of her spine. From what I have been told, *Sœur* Camilla is not the same person as the Camilla who arrived here at the abbey six years ago. When she had first arrived, Camilla was a woman at the end of her tether. She was in pieces, broken by the murder of her two-year-old son, Cole. Camilla had been washed in guilt.

Robert, a local man back in Jamaica, had approached Camilla and ordered her to take his drugs to England. This would have involved Camilla swallowing ten condoms full of cocaine, and 'delivering' them to an address in England. Camilla had refused, so Robert shot Cole. He had assumed that Camilla had more children, and planned to use Cole's death as leverage to control Camilla. He was wrong.

When Camilla had arrived at the abbey, *Sœur* Marissa had taken care of her.

Marissa had fled Chile, where she had suffered at the hands of General Pinochet's soldiers. She had come to the abbey and found her peace. Camilla had done the same, with considerable help from *Sœur* Marissa. Now it was my turn.

Sœur Camilla took another dreadlock and rubbed wax into the treated hair above it that had grown in the last month. She twisted it tightly until it became part of the dreadlock.

'Why were you crying last night?' *Sœur* Camilla asked me.

I looked at my hands, and said, 'I kept seeing them and what they were doing to me.' I touched my stomach underneath my T-shirt, and traced my fingers along the bumpy skin that had been burnt so many years ago.

'Try to keep your thoughts nice,' *Sœur* Camilla advised. 'There are many good things about your life.'

'Yeah,' I said, with not so nice thoughts in my head. I had spent years lying awake at nights, wondering when the next murder attempt would be, or if I got pregnant and how I would explain to my child who 'Daddy' was. I had been lucky. And two months ago, I took my final

HIV test, among other tests. They had all come back negative. *Sœur* Marissa called me 'blessed'.

Me? Blessed? Having decided after the first six years of violence that I had to keep moving, I had been a nomad for ten years—never staying in one place for more than six months, never trusting anyone, or even telling them my name. Until I met Hepburn. There had been something about him that made everything about him feel so safe. *Sœur* Marissa called him my 'Guardian Angel', saying he had been sent to look after me. I don't know if I believe that.

'Danica, are you awake or dreaming?' *Sœur* Camilla asked, loudly and slowly.

'Yes, I'm awake,' I replied. I had become lost in my head again.

'I have finished,' Camilla told me, screwing the lid back on the tub of hair wax, and letting it drop back into her pocket. I must have been lost in my head for some time.

'I take your mirror,' *Sœur* Camilla said, as she reached over to my bed, took hold of the mirror that lay on my bed, and handed it to me so that I could view her handiwork. I did, and liked it.

'*Sœur* Camilla, I'm scared of being bored. Of having a normal life and being bored. Of working in an office and living in a house and being bored.'

'You don't have to be bored to have a normal life,' Camilla laughed. 'Look at me. Am I bored?'

Quietly, I thought of the activities with which *Sœur* Camilla engaged her time. She hosted a youth club for the young people of this city, spoke in schools and talked with people on street corners. Her life was full and fulfilling.

'I suppose I don't have to be hit to not be bored,' I said, thinking profoundly.

Sœur Camilla nodded and said, 'I must go and prepare for my talk for tomorrow.'

'See you later, then.'

'Yes, see you later.'

Sœur Camilla left, with her black gown flowing around her as she walked. I clicked off Hepburn's cassette and dumped the paper back into the box. I had an essay to hand in to *Frère* Etienne, my history tutor.

In the stone corridor, outside of *Frère* Etienne's study, I saw the fun-loving English girl who loved to wear pink, and had a small symbol of the Cross of Jesus tattooed on her back. She had come to the abbey to do voluntary work with the local homeless people. She was looking through a tall, arched window into the courtyard, and waved at a friend who was walking along the opposite corridor, across the courtyard.

The afternoon sun threw long shadows from the monastery walls, making dark green lines stream across the grass.

From the corner of my eye, I saw François running up the staircase with a folder under his arm. I ran along the grey flagged floor of the corridor and up the pine staircase after him, calling out, 'François, François, François!'

I got to the top of the wooden staircase to see François standing there to meet me. He wasn't a monk. Like the English party girl, he was a volunteer taking time out from his comfortable life as an engineer. He had won the respect of everybody at the abbey in the way that he had adapted to working with people, instead of machines. He had discovered that people were a lot more complicated than machines, and were a lot more difficult to fix.

'What's all the fuss?' he asked.

'I just wanted to see you,' I said, quickly, with a sure and quiet smile.

He took me by the elbow and pulled me into *Sœur* Marissa's study, and left the door wide open. Just across the corridor was another open door that led onto the street outside. There were many people shuffling past hurriedly in the sunny afternoon.

In *Sœur* Marissa's study, I stood in the corner with my back against the wooden panelling. I gazed up at his broad shoulders and blond hair, and that kind face. He put his hand on my shoulder as he talked to me, making me look at the Celtic tattoo on his broad forearm that suited him so well.

I didn't hear the words he said, but I was able to just tip my head back, letting my dreadlocks be pushed up slightly by the wall, and I closed my eyes, trusting François beyond the point I trusted anyone else.

Suddenly, a stinging sensation ran through my body, as François drew closer. I stumbled forward in pain just as he kissed me softly on the lips, then pushed him away violently.

'Sorry,' François said, stepping back, and letting me cringe and swear and hit the wall. I recovered quickly. The anger evaporated.

'Let's go out,' I said.

So there we were, walking down the street, his arm around my neck and mine around his waist.

His denim jacket reminded me of something, but I could not tell him what. He'd be mortified. I walked with my head down.

'You know, you can tell me anything,' he said.

I didn't answer, although I knew this to be true. I just walked with my head down. And we carried on like that quite some time. We passed a brightly dressed middle-aged couple who sat on a bench.

The silver-haired man leant on his walking stick, and laughed as his curly-haired wife said something amusing. The sun felt pleasantly warmer on my skin as a voice told me that everything was going to be all right. Everything was going to be OK. I was still staring at the pavement we were walking on, and I asked,

'Can I tell you something?'